Ré Ó Laighléis is a writer of adult and teenage fiction in both English and Irish. His novels and short stories have been widely translated into various languages and he has been the recipient of many literary awards, including Bisto Book of the Year awards, Oireachtas awards, the North American NAMLLA Award and a European White Ravens Award. In 1998, he was presented with the 'An Peann faoi Bhláth' award by the President of Ireland, Mary McAleese, in recognition of his contribution to Irish literature. He is a former Writer-in-Residence at the National University of Ireland, Galway (2001) and held the same post with Mayo County Council in 1999.

A Dubliner by birth, he was reared in Sallynoggin and since leaving teaching in Galway in 1992 has lived in the Burren, Co. Clare.

Battle for the Burren, in manuscript form, was winner of the 2005 Oireachtas Literary Award.

By the same author

The Great Book of the Shapers: A right kick up in the Arts
(MÓINÍN, 2006)

Ecstasy and other stories (MÓINÍN, 2005)

Heart of Burren Stone (MÓINÍN, 2002)

Shooting from the Lip (compiled and edited)
(Mayo County Council, 2001)

Hooked (MÓINÍN, 1999)

Terror on the Burren (MÓINÍN, 1998)

An Nollaig sa Naigín (MÓINÍN, 2006)

Sceoin sa Bhoireann (MÓINÍN, 2005)

Gafa (MÓINÍN, 2004)

Goimh agus scéalta eile (MÓINÍN, 2004)

Bolgchaint agus scéalta eile (MÓINÍN, 2004)

Chagrin (Cló Mhaigh Eo, 1999)

Punk agus scéalta eile (Cló Mhaigh Eo, 1998)

Ecstasy agus scéalta eile (Cló Mhaigh Eo, 1998)

An Taistealaí (Cló Mhaigh Eo, 1998)

Stríocaí ar Thóin Séabra (Coiscéim, 1998)

Cluain Soineantachta (Comhar, 1997)

Aistear Intinne (Coiscéim, 1996)

Ciorcal Meiteamorfach (CIC, 1991)

Punk agus sgeulachdan eile (Trans.) (Leabhraichean Beaga, 2006)

Ecstasy agus sgeulachdan eile (Trans.) (CLÀR, 2004)

Ecstasy e altri racconti (Trans.) (MONDADORI, 1998)

Battle for the Burren

Ré Ó Laighléis

MÓINÍN

First published in 2007 by MÓINÍN
Loch Reasca, Ballyvaughan, Co. Clare, Ireland
E-mail: moinin@eircom.net
www.moinin.ie

First print 2007

A copy of this work is available in the National Library of Ireland
and in the libraries of Trinity College, Dublin, and the
constituent colleges of the National University of Ireland.

A CIP catalogue record for this book is available from the British Library.

ISBN 978-0-9554079-1-8

Set in Palatino 10.5/14pt

This book is a work of fiction set against the backdrop of historical fact.
Some names of persons and places are of those known to have existed
in 1317. All others are products of the author's imagination and, in such
instances, any resemblance to real persons, living or dead, is purely
coincidental.

A special note of thanks to Michael O'Halloran of Kildimo, Co. Limerick,
for his invaluable advice in the matter of placenames.

Cover design by Raydesign

Edited and typeset by Carole Devaney

Printed and bound in Ireland by Clódóirí Lurgan, Indreabhán, Co. na Gaillimhe

Preface

In 1317, the long-running fight for supremacy within the great Clan O'Brien was determined when the opposing sides engaged each other at Corcomroe, on the footslopes of the Burren, Co. Clare. This was the decisive battle in what has become known as 'The Wars of Turlough'. The rival cousins – Dermot, Prince of the O'Briens, and Donough, prince and leader of the Roe O'Brien faction of the clan, which had allied itself with the powerful Norman lord, de Clare – led their forces against each other in what is generally regarded as the bloodiest of all the battles fought between the sides.

Myth has it that, on the night of the eve of battle, when Donough and his men had camped by the lakeside at Loughrask, a hag of evil countenance – Dismal of the Burren – appeared to them and foretold of unprecedented slaughter in the battle that was to come. It is against this backdrop that *Battle for the Burren* is set.

This book is a work woven of the strands of the imaginative and the factual. While diligent in the historical research of the Great Battle of the O'Briens in 1317, primacy has been given to the fictional, by setting this story of love, fear and darkness in the realm of the creative. Driven by the passion of the young lovers, Iarla and Sorcha, and of the eternal struggle between Good and Evil, the reader is confronted by the forces that are the dark and sinister Feardorcha and the blind, yet visionary monk, Benignus.

Authorial licence is taken with the names of certain characters and the details of some events. Burren placenames are as known and used both then and now.

Ré Ó Laighléis
Ballyvaughan, *February 2007*

1

A day in early Autumn 1317 AD. Brother Benignus stands on the steps at the outer wall of the monastery and faces the craggy mountain which, in recent times, has borrowed its name from the settlement at Corcomroe. Abbey Hill is resplendent this day. So very resplendent is it that the morning sunshine has already managed to invade many of the secret narrow crevices that lead one deep into the dank dark caverns that form the innards of the mountain. It will be a kindly day, perhaps, Benignus thinks. Indeed, if the sunshine can win its battle against the windswept clouds that, for many days past, have rolled in in hordes above the ocean's troubled waters, it will, he thinks, be a splendidly kindly day.

He feels an itch – no, more a mixture of a tickle and an itch – play with his left ear's lobe. Instantly, he knows the touch to be a little spider. Earlier, on his way from matins in the monastery cloister, he sensed contact with a web when he had brushed against one of the rose bushes which Brother Germanus so caringly tends, when weather will allow. Benignus softly touches the earlobe, feeling gently with his fingertips to locate his friend in Nature. The little spider works his way onto the old man's hand and then the monk crouches and allows the tiny creature find the wall, then lose himself to safety in the dewy grass beneath.

Benignus' world is one of touch and taste, of sound and smell. An accident as a boy, in his home village of Trowbridge in England's Wiltshire, caused his loss of sight and so, from very early on, he has learned to negotiate the world through use of his other senses. They are his eyes and, indeed, so sharply can he use them that the other brothers acknowledge that his gift of vision is far more acutely honed than is their own. And they themselves have full use of the very organs which a simple falling from a cart has stolen from him.

"I have no need of eyes," he one time told his fellow-monks. "Seeing is of the heart and of the soul, brothers. No God as great as is our Maker would let a simple accident rob one of such a gift and fail to see him right in some other way."

Age has taught him wisdom, and wisdom patience, and it is that patience and his love of Nature and of everything that his monastic life can offer that so endears him to his Cistercian comrades. They have come here from afar to settle in the monastery of Corcomroe on the foothills of the Burren – Dál Cais' rugged rocky realm of beauty. His patience and his use of those gifts which God has left him have helped him know the world around him. Just as he knows that Abbey Hill stands a little to the east of north of him, he is equally aware that, beyond it, the bays of Aughinish and Corranroo entrap the waters of the ocean and quieten them in times of anger. So too, he knows that to the south is Turlough Hill and then Slievecarran, and furthest south of all, the magically leaning layers of Mullach Mór – the mountain kissed by God one day when He was busy in His making.

West of Moneen Valley, west of where the monks have built their abbey, stands Moneen Mountain, and, beyond that again, yet another fertile pasture that holds the townlands of Killoghill and Loughrask and several more whose names are not even known to Benignus and the others. And not far thrown from either of these two, in the area named as Muckinish, is the castle of the O'Lochlainns.

As Benignus turns from the sunshine and faces west to Moneen Mountain, all his senses tell him that there is something unusual in the breeze that wafts its way towards him. Something disturbing. A pungency of sorts. A mix of air and sweat and burning, yet no one of these is clearly identifiable on its own. It is unsettling. Even more unsettling to him now is his awareness of a sixth sense – a sense which, with his brothers, he often jokingly claims can only really be termed a fifth sense in his case. It is an awareness that, whatever the various constituents of what he smells may be, the smell itself does not bode well. He feels his nostrils swell as he takes in the odour and his feeling of discomfort is heightened as he endeavours to make meaning of it. Then, suddenly, the swishing overhead of the broad wings of a heron, flying low, distracts him momentarily and a gush of cold air follows in its wake.

"You didn't hear the bell, Benignus?"

The words of Brother Placidus deal his thinking yet another jolt.

"Brother?" Benignus says.

"The bell, my friend – did you not hear it? Come, we are about to break fast." Placidus smiles, then turns and moves back in through the arched entrance through which he had come. Benignus turns and follows, touching his way along the wooden railing as he descends the steps and favouring the grass verge of the pathway that will guide him to the entrance. As he reaches the archway, he feels the coldness

which its shadow casts upon him and a conjured image of
the flying heron fleetingly crosses his mind again. He
doubts that, in his short few years of sightedness, he had
ever seen such a bird and, if indeed he had, he certainly had
not retained any clear memory of it.

Benignus stops now, aware that the sun has been
defeated by the stone which man has built against the
elements, and yet again he draws the smell into his nostrils
and allows it swell within his lungs. He doesn't like it. No,
he most certainly does not like it.

The repeated chant of *Ora pro nobis* from within compels
him to go join his brothers.

"*Et pro cibo novo, Deo gratia.*"

"*Amen*," the brothers answer to Abbot Nilus' giving
thanks to God for the fresh food of the fields with which
the Maker has blessed their table.

Benignus sits in beside Placidus. They have been lifelong
friends, having grown up together in Trowbridge, and, at
the age of fifteen years, leaving their homeland with the
blessing of their parents and journeying far across the
water to the Cistercian Abbey of Inis Leamhnachta in the
western part of Urmhumhan, the Irish kingdom of
Ormond. It was an old travelling brother from that
monastery who had offered them the opportunity. It
presented the perfect chance for them to escape the poverty
and squalor of the peasant's life in England and, at the
same time, to gain a knowledge of scripture and of Latin.
They could never even have dreamed of such had
circumstance determined that they should have stayed at
home. And in the case of Benignus, what hope could there
be for a blind boy when he would grow to man in the

rough and tumble of the English countryside? What's more, what nobler in life for their sons than to be called by God, their parents would have thought, not to mention the lightening of the load on them that the feeding of one fewer mouth would mean.

Then, after almost thirty years together in the sister house at Inis Leamhnachta, by the pleasant flowing waters of the Suir, and despite a decree to the contrary issued by the Abbot of the mother house in Furness, the friends were asked to leave, along with four other brothers from the abbey. They were to go to join with fellow-monks from Mellifont and augment the numbers at the monastery at Corcomroe in the north of the kingdom of Thomond. And how the years had passed since then …

"You are thirsty, my Brother?"

"Yes, Placidus, very thirsty," Benignus responds. "My mind was filled with restlessness the whole night long and when I awoke I was craving water. Such was my thirst that, even during matins, I could not concentrate on prayer." And as Benignus speaks, he breaks his conversation two or three times to sip from the crude clay beaker in front of him.

Placidus, much more an earthy man than what one might term a thinker, knows that his friend's mind has been troubled for several days past. He, more than any other of the brothers, has known for years that not only is Benignus' so-called sixth sense a form of compensation for his loss of sight, but it does, in fact, bestow on him an extra dimension that helps him interpret happenings in a way not given to others. Benignus, he knows, sees beyond the obvious, beyond the physical. Sometimes, thinks Placidus, he even sees beyond this world.

"It is this trouble with the family de Clare, the Norman, isn't it, Benignus?"

His blind friend hesitates at first, but then turns towards him. "Yes, Placidus, de Clare and this treacherous ongoing liaison between his family and the Roe O'Briens against the sons of Turlough. I have seen it in the dark of night when my eyes are as closed to this earthly world as in the light of day, but when my mind is even more open than at any other time."

And Placidus looks fondly at his friend as he speaks, knowing that his gift of vision lies heavily upon him. He is just about to utter words of comfort when Benignus speaks again.

"Yes, I have seen it. There will be death and burning and carnage of a kind not seen since the time when tongues of fire and evil owned the sky and made it race in anger high above the darkened rocky mountain of Cappanawalla that is to the west of here."

Placidus' eyes widen as he listens to his friend and he feels the coldness of a shudder pass through him. Impulsively, he blesses himself, almost as if he knows that certain happenings in this world are beyond the ken of ordinary men and that, ultimately, the only defence one may have is to call upon the power of the Almighty.

"But surely, friend Benignus, if you can see such things, then it is somehow possible to avert the course of that which is to happen."

"Would that things might be so simple," replies Benignus. "There is much that can be seen, Placidus, but even the simple seer, such as I, is powerless to alter that which has been ordained by a higher being."

Placidus' mind is filled with memories of the stories he has heard since coming to the land of Burren, of the merciless destruction that had happened at Loughrask back in a pagan time, long before he, or any of his Christian brethren, had been even thought of. Before the very time of the Christ, indeed – a time when only those who had the force of might and the strength of arms and men were always seen as right. If there was truth in what Benignus saw, then there was little any could do other than that which Placidus had instinctively done some moments earlier. Again, he blesses himself and this time gives his attention to the sweet libum of oatmeal that is on the plate before him. This little loaf is to be his sustenance until work in the fields is over at day's end. Then the brothers will gather in again to share their evening meal with one another. He looks again at Benignus and the blind monk senses his friend's eyes upon him.

"Do not worry, Placidus. Understanding things as these is not in our gift and always we must surrender such to the only power that is capable of attending to them."

The abbey bell sounds once, summoning the brethren to silence as they eat. Both brothers bow their heads and taste of their loaves. As morning comes, so too will come the evening, and, should the greatest power of all will that it be so, so also will come the morrow.

2

Iarla O'Brien, son of Dermot, slaps his horse hard on the rump, sending him off at a gallop, then throws himself into the tall green fern that skirts the dirt track somewhere east of the little straggling hamlet of Ballinacragga. He quickly finds his feet again. Then, hearing horsemen, he crouches, scurries towards the cover of a nearby copse of hazels and lies belly-down against the undergrowth. The approaching steeds are surely those of his distant cousins, the Roe O'Briens, he thinks. His family has waged battle with them, on and off, for over forty years. Were they to find him on the track and to recognise him as the son of Dermot, or even worse again, grandson of the mighty Turlough, his number would be up.

Nothing of the young Iarla but the widened whites of eyes, peering through the leafy branches, is caught by the light of the full moon that hangs high above the distant shadowed stone of Eagle's Rock. His heart beats in tune with the pounding of the oncoming horses' hooves against the earth. Already he can feel the beads of sweat mounting on his chest and the coarse wool of his tunic against the heated wetness of his skin causes him to itch a little. The noise of stomping hooves is growing from pound to thunder when, suddenly, as he presses himself harder against the ground, the spindly fetlocks of the Roe O'Brien horses race like driven threads across young Iarla's view of the moon and are quickly gone again. And then, in what seems little time at all, the sound of silence is as deafening as was the noise of racing steeds.

Iarla rises gently, comes out of hiding and watches the last of the silhouetted riders take the bend close to the little harbour wall at nearby Béalaclugga, then disappear from view. The dust kicked up by the horses' hooves tickles his throat a little and he works hard to stifle the cough that, in other circumstances, he might more easily allow to come. He knows that in the clearness of the Burren air, and particularly at this time of night, sound can easily carry quite some distance and the last thing that he wants is to draw the riders back on him.

They have gone with purpose – the riders – most probably to the monks at Corcomroe, to announce the imminent arrival of the army of their leader, Prince Donough Roe O'Brien. It was Prince Donough's great ancestor, Donal Mór O'Brien, who, some generations earlier, had freely given of his land to the White Monks of the Cistercian Order to erect their edifice of stone. And so, as custom would have it, it is to be expected that Abbot Nilus will open the monastery doors in welcome to Donough and his men. If only Iarla had some way of warning his father, Dermot. He knew that, some days earlier, his father had set out from the Barony of Bunratty in the south and that, if the march had gone to plan, he and his army would this night be camped in the townland of Carron, not far from Corcomroe.

Iarla himself had left Bunratty some days before Dermot, promising when he left that he would meet up with him this very night at the Glen of Clab, just north of Carron's straggling hamlet. Reasons of battle are often noble, but, in the thinking of any young man of only nineteen years, reasons of the heart are even more so. His love for Sorcha, youngest daughter of Mahon of the Clan O'Brien – now one of his father's most bitter enemies – is as intense as it is boundless. When he thinks of her, his heart is made to race even more quickly than it had raced when earlier the horsemen had approached. Though only eighteen years of age, she is as beautiful as any ever seen and more beautiful than most. Sorcha is tall and fair and gentle, and the only cloud that hangs over the young lovers is that their fathers – like their fathers' fathers – cannot see eye to eye.

And so, Iarla's early departure had been made so that he could meet up with his lovely Sorcha. Like every other meeting they had had, this one too was to be done in greatest secrecy. Were either of the chieftains to learn of this love, the young couple would be compelled to end their relationship or, in Iarla's case, to forego all future rights of succession to Dermot's kingdom. For two years past, since first they had begun to see each other, they had secretly met in different places within Mahon's lands. The first time they had kissed was a day when they had walked hand in hand through a verdant pasture near to where Sorcha's father's lands meet the sometimes gentle, sometimes violent ocean. And when they touched, lips on lips, it was as though all of life had opened to them and there could be nothing for them everafter but happiness and joy. After that, their meetings became many, always secret, and each and every one of them arranged through friends and emissaries whom they knew to be trustworthy.

But tonight's meeting of the lovers had been the most daring by far, done as it was on the eve of their fathers' going to battle, one against the other. Indeed, Iarla himself would take the field and stand shoulder to shoulder alongside Dermot and face – and, if necessary, kill – the father of the woman whom he loves. For some weeks now the young couple had known the time and place of battle, and Sorcha, as a pretence, had got her father to agree that she could travel with him on his march to join Prince Donough, so that she could visit her mother's people in the quarter known as Muckinish, just a little to the north of the townlands of Killoghill and Loughrask.

"Iarla," she whispered, as she saw the lithe athletic figure of her loved one pass through the tree-lined passageway that led down from Killoghill to the banks of the little lake of Loughrask. Iarla turned, his half-face caught in moonlight as he did so, and saw the beautiful Sorcha nestled by a tree trunk which he had already passed. She was fair of skin and radiant in her elegance, and the selfsame light of moon which had played with his own face revealed her to him in all her shapeliness and beauty.

"Sorcha," he said, and immediately moved towards her and took her in his arms. He held her tightly, could feel her heart race fiercely against his chest. Then he eased her back from him, allowing the moonlight dance again on the beauty of her face.

"Sorcha," he repeated, then drew her to him once again, "I have missed you so much."

Their pressing of themselves body against body, face on face, mouth on mouth, made them wish they could be one.

"I've missed you too, my Iarla," panted Sorcha, drawing back a little and loosening the thong in the bodice of her dress. She moved her face to find his lips again and they kissed hard and long. Then she drew his mouth down onto her open breast. And in their intimacy, as their passion poured and they made one of themselves, no further from them than that number of paces one might count upon a single hand, the bushes parted, almost unnoticeably. And for a time, dark and furtive unknown eyes looked out upon them in their union.

And, in passion's wake, as the lovers lay resting, one against the other, a cold breeze crept, gently at first, then suddenly swept in even harder from the ocean, carrying with it clouds that were thick and black and heavy. The young couple raised their eyes and saw the broad dark blanket begin to make nothing of the host of stars that had adorned the clear night sky. They stood, as of yet contained in their alarm, brushing twigs and leaves from themselves while rearranging their various items of clothing. And by the lake, down near the sheltered spot where Prince Donough and his men had camped, the horses grew quite restless and, on the rising breeze, Iarla and Sorcha could hear their neighing clearly. The breeze grew even stronger again, then into wind, and then the largest light of all – that of the moon – was in danger of occlusion.

"Iarla," said Sorcha, drawing his attention to the sky again. The tone of her voice carried in it a mixture of anxiety and fear. And as the lovers watched, they saw the vile and evil blackness of a cloud inch its way into the ball of light and put an end to shadows on the earth below. And for some seconds, as the young couple stood together tightly, an eerie stillness ruled the world a while. No longer the sound of wind or breeze, no horses neighing, no beat of lovers' hearts one against the other.

Silence. Then, slowly from the bowels of the firmament overhead, came the sound of a thunder – round and rolled and rumbling. It was as though it had at first been issued from the innards of the earth and had somehow made its way onto a higher plane. Sorcha nestled ever closer to her young man. The lovers lowered their gaze and looked in trepidation at each other and, as they did so, a flash of light – more blue than it was yellow – crossed the angry sky and cast an eerie world of shadow on their faces. Then suddenly, the neighing again of horses by the lakeside, this time peppered with the shouting of Prince Donough's men. And as suddenly again, despite the cloud-filled sky, a light was cast over the area of the lake and, for the first time on this night, Iarla could see the faces of many of the men against whom he would do battle on the morrow. They were faces filled with horror and, despite the apparent absence of assailants, many of their number were red and raw and bloodied. Their shouts by now had turned to screams and then to cries of terror, and some of Prince Donough's army made for the water and threw themselves headlong into the miry lake. Others were busy in their efforts to restrain the horses. The animals seemed so fired with anger that the brown and bulbous eyes in their large heads threw back the mysterious light which had been cast upon them.

"There," cried one of Prince Donough's men from below in the camp, and he seemed to point to the place where the young lovers stood, and then, along with some of his fellow-soldiers, make in their direction. Sorcha's eyes widened.

"Go, Iarla, go. And may God keep you safe for me tomorrow."

Iarla looked at Sorcha. She was so beautiful, even when the elements played evil tricks and cast winding shadows on her face. But this, he knew, was not a time to dwell on thoughts of beauty.

"He will. He will keep me safe for you, my Sorcha, and when tomorrow's fight is over, we will be together, no matter what." He kissed her hard and, in his heart, wanted nothing but to kiss her more. But Sorcha could hear the shouts of the oncoming soldiers. She pushed him from her.

"Go, Iarla. For the love of God, go." She held him out from her and they looked firmly at each other.

"I love you," he said. Then he was gone, heading for the safety of Killoghill's trees and from there, in time, onto the loose limestone scree spurned from their downslopes by the mountains that are Moneen and the lesser Sliabh na gCapall. Her eyes followed him in his going and, as they did, those of Feardorcha, the Roe O'Brien lieutenant who, all this time, had watched the lovers in their intimacy, fastened hard and ominously onto Sorcha's shape as she tightened the bodice of her dress. Then, from amidst the bushes, the dark lieutenant emitted a sinister and low-pitched growl that seemed, if anything, more animal than human.

When Iarla reached the higher ground, he looked back towards the lake. The sky by now had fully cleared again and he could see that whatever it was that had caused the earlier disturbance in the camp, it had been abated. The horses had been gathered in again and, though some were busy tending to the number of their comrades who had been mysteriously injured, things otherwise had seemed to return to their previous normality. Despite his distance from the lake, he thought he could discern the form of Sorcha sitting with her father, Mahon, next to Prince Donough himself.

And so, by the time that Iarla had approached Ballinacragga on this night that had already been a mixture of passion and strange happenings, he was still at odds to know who were the marauders on Prince Donough's camp. Indeed, he was even more at odds to understand the tricks with light and dark that Nature seemed to play. He did, however, have the ease of mind of knowing that his lovely Sorcha was safe. And then, when he heard Prince Donough's horse-soldiers on the track, all but survival was instantly banished from his mind. Into the fern, head down and let them pass, as he had done.

Half-hunched now, Iarla scurries across the road and slithers down into the ditch that runs along the mountainy side of the track. He moves stealthily on his way, safely reaching the point where the horse-soldiers have already turned off for the monastery at Corcomroe. He stops and carefully eases his head above the edge of the ditch. There is torchlight to be seen at the distant abbey. The chill of night combines with the wetness of the fern in which he has been lying and he feels the one-time heated perspiration turn to coldness on his chest. His horse is long gone by now and there is nothing for him but to travel on foot. He lowers his head again and moves quickly along the ditch. He knows this route will take him safely to the Glen of Clab and to his father.

3

Brother Benignus' day of restlessness has carried on into the time of darkness and, even further then, into his sleep beyond the midnight hour. And as he sleeps, his inner eye has seen all that has happened by Loughrask's lonely lake – all and even more. The secret meeting of the young lovers in the leafy passageway above the lake, the strange and temperamental playing of Nature with the elements, the disturbance of the horses and the despair-filled faces of Prince Donough's soldiers. But, clearest of all, what blind Benignus sees is prophecy fulfill itself. Not since before the time of Christ – the selfsame Christ to whom Benignus has devoted his whole life – has the evil hag, who has long been said to haunt the lakeshore at Loughrask, been known to have appeared. It had been in the time of savagery, some two hundred years before the coming of the Saviour, that the dark and vicious Barbey had unleashed their wrath on the kindly folk who once settled by Loughrask. And when the slaughter had been done, so it was told, it was then that, from the burning embers of the battle, rose up a figure dark and hideous to the eye – a hag of evil countenance who confronted the good and blessed Sobharthan, then seer of Loughrask, and left the scene of destruction with her foreboding promise of return.

And in his dream this night, some fifteen hundred years since that promise had been made, the monk Benignus sees that which has caused men to tremble and to throw themselves into the reed-filled quagmire that is sometimes lake and sometimes not. What she has spoken to Prince Donough reveals itself most ugly to the blind old man: *'I am Dismal of the Burren and I am of the Tuatha Dé Danann, and I declare that your head and the heads of your army will be lost. Proudly as you move to the battlefield, the time is not far when all but a few of you will be slain.'*

And in Benignus' sleep, the hag, Dismal of the Burren, looks deep into the brightness of his eyes and the old monk sees her ugliness and her evil. To his seer's eye she is distorted and loathsome, most hideous to look upon. Her face, worn and withered, is a bluish-grey and her coarse and tangled hair is like the shredded strands of a tunic made of sackcloth. She nears him with the long bent nails of her raised and crooked hand and, as she does so, Benignus suddenly bolts upright on the cold stone slab on which his nights of little sleep are spent. His eyes cast light onto the darkness of his meagre cell and he hears the pounding of the horsemen on the wooden door of the monastery. Dismal is gone now, but, in his heart, Benignus knows that the soul of any who has seen her and has survived is filled with a blackness as dark and ugly as the soul of Dismal herself. He hears the sandled feet of his fellow-brothers scurry through the passageway outside his cell as they hasten towards the monastery door.

"No, don't open," cries Benignus aloud, "don't open."

But as his words of warning reverberate within his tight stone cell, he hears the loosening of the massive iron bolts and the removal of the three mighty wooden beams that secure the door against the dangers of invasion. Then, within seconds, the monastery bell is sounded and the brothers know that they must convene with urgency in the

Each and every one of them has devoted his life to God and, in so doing, has committed himself to love and peace. Feardorcha has perceived the brethren's disgruntlement and is quick in his resolve to quell it before it has either time or opportunity to seethe and swell in their holy minds.

"In the early hours to come, Prince Donough and his army will march here from their encampment at Loughrask. We will need quarters for our officers and our animals. Our infantry will camp in the gardens within the monastery walls."

Feardorcha's speech has no element of request in it. Neither has he thought that what he says might be in any way contested, especially now that he is more forceful in his presentation. And, though the brethren's minds are anxious at what they hear, there is only one amongst them who thinks to stand up to this lieutenant of Prince Donough's.

"This is the house of God," Benignus says. His speech is, as ever, gentle, yet audible to all. Once again Feardorcha scans the gathering of brothers standing out before him. He cannot discern which of them it is who has spoken.

"This is the house of God," the old monk says again, "not a place to be defiled by those whose only intention is to inflict harm upon their fellow-men."

The other brothers look towards Benignus. Though quiet still, in their hearts they are happy that some one of their number has had the courage to openly declare what they themselves are feeling. None but Abbot Nilus is disquieted by Benignus' stand against the intruders and that itself is only because he is charged with the burden of responsibility for all that happens within the hallowed walls. Feardorcha, who by now has identified the speaker, winces and looks disapprovingly in Benignus' direction. His eyes narrow into slits of anger as he stares down at the old man. Beneath his breastplate his chest is heaving and he can feel his blood pulsate its way ever faster through his veins. How dare this old brother who knows nothing of the world defy him in this way, he thinks.

"Come here, Brother," Feardorcha bids Benignus.

Placidus, who all this time is by his old friend's side, takes hold of Benignus' arm and quietly bids him stay where he is. Feardorcha, seeing this and fearing even more defiance, this time bellows out his instruction.

"Here, old man – now."

"It's all right, Placidus," Benignus tells his friend, as he pats the hand that is restraining him. "I will come to little harm." And Benignus begins to gently make his way in the direction of the rostrum. As he moves, Feardorcha eases the semi egg-shaped iron helmet from his head. The metal noseband slithers upwards towards his forehead as he removes the covering, revealing a long and narrow Norman nose – almost as long, indeed, as is the noseband itself. Now, visible to all but blind Benignus, of course, is Feardorcha's close-knit mail headdress. Its thousands of small iron rings are so closely bound together that, at a distance, one would almost think it a fashioned sheet of metal. Feardorcha, still waiting for Benignus to reach him, clenches his right fist inside his mail glove, then presses it hard into the palm of his other hand.

Benignus now stands before the horseman, his face benign and kindly.

"What was it you said, monk?" asks Feardorcha. No use of 'brother' this time when the soldier speaks to him. The derision in his speech is plain to all, most particularly to Benignus himself. And yet the old man smiles and the searing yellow flame of the surrounding torchlight is mellowed in the whiteness of his eyes.

"Brother Feardorcha," begins Benignus, "I am simply reminding you that the house in which we stand is the house of –" and, as Benignus speaks, Feardorcha sweeps his mail-clad hand hard across the old man's face, knocking him to the ground. The other monks back away in shock and, as they do so, the horsemen rush forward and form a barrier between them and the place where Feardorcha stands.

"Shut it, monk," Feardorcha says. Benignus tries to rise again, but as he does, Feardorcha comes forward and stomps down hard on the old brother's hand. The sound of bones crunching beneath the weight of the lieutenant's foot makes the onlooking brethren cringe.

"Please," cries Abbot Nilus, as he makes his way towards the prince's envoy, "this is not –"

And with that, he too is met with the sweeping backhand of the leader of the horsemen and is sent sprawling into the body of the dining hall.

"Shut it, I said."

Then Feardorcha turns again to face Benignus. The blind man is groping on the ground, not knowing whether to attend to his bleeding cheek or to the crushed bones in his hand. The soldier comes forward once again and is just about to kick the old man as he rises when Benignus turns his head to face him and the bright whiteness of his eyes is projected as a light most brilliant onto Feardorcha's face. For a moment, it is as though Feardorcha is paralysed in his movement and then the light that has been cast upon his countenance recedes and is buried once again deep behind the old monk's eyes.

Feardorcha is obviously shaken. He cannot contend with whatever this power that the old man has might be, cannot understand it. Indeed, it is obvious from the looks on the faces of the other horsemen that they too cannot interpret what they are seeing. Only the monks can understand. They know that Benignus' inner soul has been touched by God and that he has been sometimes blessed, yet sometimes cursed, with the powers that go with his gift of vision. Feardorcha backs away, trying to gather himself and to make sense of this strangeness that has happened. He is by the rostrum once again, looking towards Benignus when he notices an even stranger thing: the cut which his sweeping blow had inflicted on the old monk's cheek is gone. Not only that, but Benignus now shows no sign whatsoever of there being anything awry with his hand – the same hand upon which Feardorcha had so deliberately trodden. Feardorcha squirms. He knows only one answer to this challenge to his supremacy.

"Take him away from me and lock him in his cell," he orders and, within seconds, a number of Feardorcha's men have ushered Benignus from the hall.

"We will need quarters, Abbot," Feardorcha continues, somewhat less confidently than had earlier been the case. His face now is a ghostly white and it is obvious that, despite getting the upper hand on Benignus in one respect, he is still a little shaken by what has passed. Nilus, thinking first and foremost of the safety of his brothers, simply bows his head a little as he looks at Feardorcha.

"As you wish, Master Feardorcha," he says. "They will be readied for your purpose."

Over the years, all of the monks have come to know of the conspiracy of the Roe O'Briens with the Norman lord de Clare and of the injustices they have inflicted on the people of the Clan of Turlough. And so, many of the brethren now feel anger towards their Abbot that he should make the monastery available to Prince Donough and his men. But others can appreciate the no-win bind in which Nilus finds himself. Most ironic of all, perhaps, is that the only overt resistance to the soldiers has come from the blind and feeble Benignus.

Though back in his quarters now, Benignus has heard most of what has passed since he has been taken from the dining hall. In the still night air, all that Feardorcha has said has been carried to him through the bars of the window in his cell. His mind is troubled. Much of what there is to come is clearer to him than was earlier the case. He sees things of Iarla, the son of Dermot, and his young love Sorcha, and of the occupation of the monastery by the forces of Prince Donough. But most troublesome of all is his vision of destruction. He squeezes his eyelids tightly as if to exorcise all that he can see, yet knows that he will sleep but very little on this troubled night.

4

The horses stir excitedly where they are tied in line at the outskirts of Dermot O'Brien's encampment at the Glen of Clab. For several minutes past, their ears have been cocked as they listened to the rustling amongst the hazel copses to the northern side of the camp. Their hearing is so much sharper than that of their keeper, but now their restlessness has also alerted him to the sound of movement out there in the bushes. The keeper is young – thirteen, fourteen years of age at most. He is glad to have been trusted by his chieftain to watch over the horses, yet he is nervous. Darkness and the fear of what he cannot see has added to his nervousness. He moves amongst the horses, looking out into the hazel bushes. All he can see is the silvery backs of the leaves as the moonlight catches them, yielding to the breeze.

"Don't move, don't speak, don't scream," a voice says threateningly from behind him, as an arm closes tightly around the youth's neck. The boy feels the point of a dagger against his cheek. His heart jumps in shock and he whimpers like a puppy dog. His eyes are big and round and fear-filled, and he can feel his legs buckling beneath him. Even if he did decide to scream, it is doubtful that he would be able to do so. Then he feels an easing of the pressure on his neck and he is swung around to face the intruder.

"Master Iarla," he says, his bulging eyes relieved to see that what he had thought to be a marauder is none other than his chieftain's son. Then Iarla bursts out laughing.

"Fionnán, Fionnán, Fionnán," he says, as he begins to control his laughter, "I have been out there for the last five minutes just wondering what it was going to take to make you notice that there was a stirring in the bushes."

Fionnán is gathering himself a little and, by now, he is less shaken than he is angry. But even his anger is quickly overridden by the realisation that he is still in one piece. Now he too bursts into laughter.

"Good on you, Fionnán, good on you," says Iarla, firmly shaking the shoulder of his younger clansman as he speaks, and now he can see the last traces of nervousness vanish from his face. "There is nothing more out there for now. Nothing will stir until we break camp in the morning and head for Corcomroe."

Iarla purposely tells him this in order to dispel any vestige of anxiety the boy may still feel. Thinking back on it, he knows that coming from the bushes as he did may not have been all that wise in terms of putting Fionnán at his ease and the last thing he wishes to do is to leave the youngster chasing shadows the whole night long. With that thought foremost in his mind, he decides to make no mention of having seen Prince Donough's riders earlier in the night.

"I will send you up some gruel from the cauldron," Iarla tells him, as he moves away and makes towards the encampment.

"That would be most welcome, Master Iarla, most welcome," says Fionnán, and he blows into his cupped hands, vigorously rubbing them together. Then Iarla disappears into yet another copse of hazel bushes and makes for the camp.

Even before Iarla emerges from the hazels he can hear his father's voice as he discusses the morrow's strategies with his officers. Dermot O'Brien stops speaking as he sees his son come towards him. The chieftain stands and his officers turn to see who is approaching.

"Iarla," says Dermot, and he comes forward, embraces his son, then places an arm across his shoulder and directs him towards the campfire. "Come sit with us. We are discussing tomorrow's march north. What news from there, if any?"

Iarla thinks quickly. It might not be wise of him to say too much of what he has seen in front of his father's officers. It is, he thinks, best left until their meeting has broken up and they have gone to their beds. Then he will take the opportunity to sit a little longer with his father and tell him of what he has seen earlier in the night.

The battle briefing continues for some time. There are few within the gathering who do not have a blood tie with the O'Briens. These men around the campfire have come, out of allegiance, from the many far-flung corners of Thomond. There are MacNamaras, MacClancys, even some Ó Dálaighs in their midst, and many others bearing names that are not these. Many of them are men who have soldiered side by side with Dermot in the past, while others are much younger men who will carry with them into battle the duty that family tradition places on them. But common to them all, whether young or old, is a willingness to fight in defence of the honour of their kinsfolk. And when discussion's done, the officers retire to bed, none knowing how many of their number will even be alive to do so again on the following night.

Dermot and Iarla sit opposite each other at the fire, the father jabbing a half-pared blackthorn stick at the huge log which has been burning all night long beneath the blackened cauldron of gruel. The son watches the reflected light of the flames make dancing shadows on his chieftain-father's face.

"So, Iarla, what of the north?" asks Dermot, not shifting his gaze from the flaming log.

"There is much movement there. Feardorcha of the Roe O'Briens has taken a contingent of Prince Donough's cavalry to Corcomroe this night."

"Hmm, Feardorcha! I should have known he would involve himself. Donough has probably promised him some of our lands when the battle is over," says Dermot, and he jabs the log even more forcefully with the blackthorn stick. "Always a man with an eye for quick gain is the same Feardorcha."

Iarla remains silent. He can see the signs of worry in his father's face and knows that he does not in the least relish confronting so sinister a foe in the battle that is to come.

"The riders," says Dermot, "were they many?"

"Thirty, maybe thirty-five."

"Hmm! Just an advance party so. They've probably been sent to secure the abbey for Donough's forces."

"But, surely, father, the monks will not allow it."

"I wish that it were so, my son, but I fear that Abbot Nilus will have little choice but to make the holy monastery available to them. It is either that or meet the same end that many of our number will have met on the foothills of the Burren by the time that darkness closes on another day."

Then there is silence for several seconds. The ominous tone in his father's voice unsettles Iarla a little. He is aware that he has said nothing yet of the strange things he has seen by the lake at Loughrask earlier in the night. Indeed, were he to mention it, how could he possibly explain what he had been doing there? The eve of battle would hardly seem the best of times to tell his father of the relationship that he and Sorcha have developed. And if his father were to know that this relationship had been going on for the past two years, God only knows how he might react. But Iarla's duty as a chieftain's son compels him to share with his father that which he has learned. He knows that, in the morning, not long after the sun creeps over Abbey Hill, the lives of many of his kinsmen could be lost and if there is any piece of information that can lessen the number that might fall, then he should divulge it to his father.

"I was over in Muckinish and down as far as the townland of Loughrask in my travels, father," Iarla begins tentatively.

"Muckinish and Loughrask! What in the name of God took you over that way?"

How dearly Iarla would like to tell his father the truth of what had taken him there, but he knows that he cannot do so.

"I was visiting the Red O'Donoghues." This was not a lie. Iarla had, earlier in the day, visited his distant cousins near the townland of Killoghill, but that, of course, was the lesser part of his business.

"Ah, your mother will be pleased. She has a great fondness for her O'Donoghue cousins. How is the old man?"

"He is weak, nearing death, I fear. He will not be with us for tomorrow's deeds."

Dermot does not reply. He simply nods in resignation and knows he can do nothing but accept that a loyal kinsman who often in the past had stood beside him on the field of battle will not be there for this, the greatest of all frays. Iarla is still trying to think of a way to relate what he has seen at Loughrask when his father speaks again.

"Is the lake at Loughrask swelled with water these times?"

For an instant, Iarla is taken aback by his father's question. It is, he thinks, almost as if Dermot could read his thoughts. But then, just as quickly again, he realises that this gives him the perfect opportunity to tell what he has seen without volunteering any information concerning Sorcha.

"Yes, father, it is very high."

Dermot looks towards the sky and sees the fullness of the fresh new moon. "Of course," he says, "there is a spring tide this past few days." Again a silence, again the awkwardness for Iarla of knowing that he must tell his father of the strange things he has seen on the banks of Loughrask's tidal turlough.

"Prince Donough and his forces have camped there for the night, father."

"Yes," says Dermot, "so the MacNamara scouts informed us when they arrived to meet us here tonight. They had travelled the high track nearer to the ocean and could see the enemy's fires burning down by the lake."

News that Dermot already knew of the encampment at Loughrask unsettles Iarla a little more. He had thought that he might offer that information as a way of easing himself into telling his father of the more sinister happenings he had witnessed.

"You know, father, when I was there above the shores of Loughrask, a strange thing happened."

"Strange! In what way strange?"

"Well, one minute, the night was calm and the sky above was clear. Then, suddenly, a sheet of darkness drew itself across the stars and stole the moon from the sky and, as it did so, a rumble and a rolling rattled all around."

As Dermot listens, dark shadows fill the lines the years have etched into his face. His brow tightens and his eyes fix firmly on his son as he tells what he has seen.

"And then, out of the darkness of the night, a blinding flashing light appeared, almost as if it wasn't of this world, and it cast itself onto Prince Donough's men. There was no sign of marauders and yet the faces of Prince Donough's soldiers were clearly bloodied and filled with fear." Iarla pauses.

"Yes, yes, go on, son. What else?"

Iarla takes time to draw his breath. He himself has not had the opportunity to think seriously on what he had seen earlier and it is only now, as he tells his father of these happenings, that he begins to realise how very strange they really are.

"His soldiers ran headlong for the lake and threw themselves into its murky waters and, as we looked on –"

"We! You were not alone, then?"

"What?" asks Iarla, startled at having made this slip.

"There was someone with you, son?"

"Yes, yes. My horse. I had ridden down the passage

from Killoghill to Loughrask," says Iarla, glad that, despite being caught off guard a little, he still has the presence of mind to think of this.

"What then?"

"Well, it's strange, but then everything just quietened once again and it was as if none of what had been observed had happened at all."

Dermot sits pensively for several seconds, his eyes focused on the great log that still burns between them. Iarla watches the reflection of the yellow flames in his father's eyes.

"It is the prophecy, the ancient prophecy of Sobharthan and of those who passed the gift of vision on to her. It is a sign that it is bearing fruit," says Dermot. There is a gravity in his voice and a sense of the foreboding.

"Prophecy, father? Sobharthan? Who is Sobharthan?"

Dermot raises the stick with which he has been poking the fire and he stares intently at its reddened tip. Iarla can tell to look at him that he is gathering his thoughts before speaking. The chieftain picks carefully at the charred end of the rod, then looks directly into his son's eyes.

"It is a long and ancient story, and probably not even true. But it has lasted all the years and I suspect that it has been so added to here and there that, as it stands now, it may bear little or no resemblance to what the original telling may have been." Dermot stops, not showing any real signs that he intends to tell the tale to which he has alluded.

"Well, father?"

"Well, what?"

"The story."

"Uh, I'm not sure that I can even begin to remember it in any detail. It is so long since I myself have heard it."

Iarla looks at him imploringly with the big wide eyes with which, as a young child, he used to so easily get around his father. Fond memories of those times cause Dermot to smile.

"Stop it, stop it," says Dermot.

But Iarla can tell that this protestation is less than forceful.

"Please, father."

The smile widens on the chieftain's lips. "All right, all right, all right," he says, feigning a reluctant surrender, but secretly he is as happy as his son to have the opportunity to relive a habit of old. Dermot lays down the blackthorn stick, sits back a second or two to gather his thoughts and then leans in towards the fire again.

"It was before the time of Our Dear Lord and Saviour, Jesus Christ. Indeed, some two hundred years before His time, if what is told is truth. A family from some Nordic land had come to settle in Loughrask. Even before their coming to the place, it was said that the area around the lake was haunted by the spirit of a hideous and evil hag. In time, the leader of this Nordic clan, the warrior Emlik, married Orla, a kinswoman of the Celtic chieftain Cneasán, and amongst the children born of their union was a daughter, Sobharthan. Sobharthan was a child both blessed and cursed, for she was made to carry in her person the gift of vision. She was a seer and her gift had been born of a goodness which, if there be honesty and truth in what is told, was intended to fight the eternal battle against the evil that was embodied in the hag of Loughrask."

Iarla titters as his father reaches this point in his telling.

"Yes," says Dermot, "it has always seemed a very far-fetched story to me too and yet, in my childhood, the old people used to put great stock in it."

"What of Sobharthan then, father? If she was supposed to fight the eternal battle against Evil, where is she now?"

"That is precisely what is interesting about what you have reported having seen tonight, my son."

"How do you mean?"

"Well, all those years ago, back before the time of Christ, it is said that a ferocious battle was fought at Loughrask and that, when everyone was slain, the belly of the lake opened wide and swallowed all, deep into the darkened bowels of the earth."

Iarla's eyes are wide with wonder as his father tells him this. "All?" he asks.

"All. All, that is, except for the hag and Sobharthan. It is said that Evil and Good will live on to do battle on another day."

"So," says Iarla, "that is the prophecy?"

"Well, yes, in part. But what disturbs me about what you have seen tonight is that, at the time of the destruction of the Clan of Emlik, even more was prophesied."

"More?"

"Yes, it was foretold then that when cousins would march against each other to do battle at a holy place on the foothills of the Burren, one of their armies would camp by the lake at Loughrask in advance of battle. It was said that the hag, known as Dismal of the Burren, would appear again and that that reappearance would presage a destruction on a scale not seen since the time of Emlik and his people."

Iarla is inclined to laugh, but the seriousness in his

father's face prevents him from doing so.

"Do you mean, father, that that which I have seen tonight is –"

"Who knows, who knows! I cannot even be sure myself that there is any truth in there ever having been a hag. Indeed, the good Lord knows that any hag with an interest in keeping herself warm wouldn't go within an ass's roar of so damp and wretched a spot as Loughrask."

This latter comment is Dermot's way of undoing any uneasiness his telling of this story may have generated. It brings a smile to Iarla's lips and then full laughter.

"Not at all, son. It's a yarn, an ould wives' tale, as the Saxons are wont to term such things."

Then they each laugh heartily, seemingly dismissing both the events of the night itself and the story which Dermot has related as being of no importance.

"Come on, lad, away to bed with you. You'll need all your strength for what's to come," says Dermot, and he slaps his son on the back, then watches him make for the sleeping quarters.

Dermot turns towards the fire again and removes the cauldron from the metal crossbar from which it has hung for several hours past, then places it to one side. He raises a bucket of water that has been nearby since earlier in the night and throws the liquid over the burning log. He works his foot against the remains of the fire, scattering any embers that may have survived the dousing. Then he too turns and makes for his bed.

Young Iarla lies flat on his back, facing the infinity of the stars above. Thoughts of Sorcha come to his mind and bring a sense of warmth with them. The notion that within a year or so they might be married is a comfort to him. If only they could find a way of getting their fathers to settle their longstanding differences. Then his thinking turns to the events of the night, from the happenings at the lake to the evil portent of Feardorcha and his riders making for the sanctuary of Corcomroe. He smiles as he thinks of the fright that he had given poor Fionnán when he crept up on him. Fionnán, he thinks, then bolts upright in his bed. He has totally forgotten that he had promised to have a bowl of gruel sent up to him. Iarla grabs his tunic, pulls it over his head again and makes back for the campfire.

When Dermot's son reaches the campfire, he finds only the ashes which his father has scattered. Here and there, there is still an ember which, despite both Dermot's and the water's efforts, still glows against the blackness of the earth. Iarla, however, is not relying on the embers for light. The sky above is clear and already his eyes have adjusted well to all that is around him. He locates the cauldron with ease, raises the iron ladle from its belly and fills a bowl of gruel for the young keeper of the horses. There is heat in it still, despite its earlier removal from the flame. He cups the bowl in both hands and moves towards the bushes.

"Fionnán, Fionnán," Iarla calls softly from amongst the hazels. He is aware of not coming on the youngster without warning for a second time. There is no answer. He has fallen asleep already, thinks Iarla, and sure, why not? Nothing will happen until morning.

"Fionnán," he calls again, and still no answer. He is annoyed at himself that he had forgotten to fulfill his promise to the young lad. Iarla turns back towards the camp and, as he does so, he trips over a little mound which is half-concealed beneath one of the bushes, spilling the contents of the bowl of gruel on the ground.

"*Mallacht air,*" he says aloud, cursing his carelessness. He gathers himself, then bends to pick up the bowl when what little light there is catches something white sticking out from the underside of the hazel bush. He lowers himself even further then and, to his amazement, finds that what he sees is an arm. Quickly he parts the lower branches of the bush and follows the arm up to the shoulder, then decides to pull whoever it is who lies beneath the foliage out into a clearing. Iarla's eyes widen as it becomes all too apparent to him that it is Fionnán.

"Fionnán, Fionnán," he says, with much more urgency in his voice this time than was earlier the case. Once in the clearing and with the benefit of extra visibility, he lowers himself by the young man's side only to see the broken stem of an arrow protruding from Fionnán's temple. Iarla's eyes widen, their whites catching the light of the moon. The arrowhead is deep within the skull and it is long past the point where anything can be done to assist his young kinsman. The horses, thinks Iarla, and he swiftly moves away from Fionnán and races through the bushes to the place where the horses had been tied. Gone! Gone on the very eve of battle. The portents do not augur well, he thinks.

"Father," he screams, then bolts back through the bushes and makes for the encampment once again.

5

"But, please, he is a blind old man –"

"I don't give a damn if he's deaf, dumb and blind, get him out of the cell. I have need of a place to sleep."

"But, Master Feardorcha, he is feeble and far too –"

"Out, I said, or am I expected to sleep beneath the elements on the eve of doing battle?" And as Feardorcha barks this at Nilus, he knocks the Abbot to the floor, pushes in the door of Brother Benignus' cell and barges into the little stone quarters. He sweeps the lighted torch that he is bearing across the breadth of the cell, but there is no sign of the elderly brother.

"Monk!" he bellows.

"Feardorcha," a voice says calmly from a corner of the cell.

Prince Donough's emissary is startled when he hears the voice behind him. He turns and threateningly thrusts the flaming torch in the direction from which the words have come.

"Monk, I want you out of …"

Feardorcha stops mid-sentence when he sees the lighted eyes of Brother Benignus. They are white, whiter than the whitest thing that Feardorcha can ever remember seeing, whiter than the pale face of the old monk which stands out against the greyness of the fissured stone. Feardorcha is momentarily fixed to the spot on which he stands but, suddenly, he lunges forward with the bullrush torch and makes to jab at the face of the old man. Benignus moves his head to one side and, with bewildering speed, raises his hand, grabs hold of the head of the lighted bullrush and pulls Feardorcha towards him. Their noses almost touch.

"You want for something, Master Feardorcha?" Benignus asks, his white blind eyes unnerving the younger man.

Beads of sweat are dropping from the tip of Feardorcha's nose and he is totally unsettled by the old man's presence. He cannot believe that this feeble monk could have the strength to pull him to him in this fashion. His eyes flit from Benignus' face to the hand which has seized the flaming bullrush. The yellow flames violently weave their way up through the openings between Benignus' fingers and engulf his hand in fire. My God! How is it not burning the old monk's hand, Feardorcha wonders. Just then, Abbot Nilus, who by now has regained his footing outside the cell, enters the chamber, eager to protect his older comrade.

"Please, Master Feardorcha, leave Brother Benignus to his –"

Impulsively, Feardorcha wrenches the torch from Benignus' grasp and makes to plunge it into the Abbot's face. But, even more speedily, the blind old monk shouts, "No, Feardorcha," and the soldier turns back to face the Brother. Benignus quickly reaches his left hand forward and presses his palm hard against the intruder's forehead. Instantly Feardorcha is inexplicably immobilised. Though he does not drop the torch, it dips limply towards the floor and he himself falls to his knees in front of the holy man.

"Benignus," says Abbot Nilus, his voice filled with anxiety.

"It is all right, my Brother Nilus, he will come to little harm."

As Feardorcha has fallen to his knees, Benignus has kept his palm pressed against the emissary's forehead. Now he removes his hand and there, clearly burnt into the centre of the soldier's forehead, is the form of the crucifix. Despite the fact that Nilus is aware of Benignus' gift of vision and that he has other powers besides, he is, nonetheless, taken aback when he sees this.

"It is best you go now, Brother," Benignus tells his superior. Nilus stands in the doorway of the cell for several seconds, still shaken by what it is that he has witnessed and pondering the wisdom of leaving Benignus and Feardorcha together.

"Go, Brother," repeats Benignus, "there is no danger here for me." The Abbot looks at his fellow-brother, bows, then backs out of the cell and stands outside the door.

Benignus moves across the cell and stands by the barred window. Feardorcha is still on his knees, docile, seemingly numbed by whatever it is that Benignus has done to him.

"You had wished to speak with me, Master Feardorcha."

Mention of his name seems to jolt the soldier from his inertia. "Brother?" he asks.

"You had wished to speak with me for some reason?"

Feardorcha raises his hand to his forehead. He can feel an intense warmth across his brow. But the cross, which only moments earlier had been burnt into his skin, has vanished. Not even the slightest trace of it ever having been there remains. The soldier seems not to know exactly where he is or what has been his purpose in barging into Benignus' quarters.

"No. No, Brother, I had no wish to speak with you." His
eyes are lowered as he speaks, his speech morose. It is as
though what he says is uttered without feeling.

"Then I think it best that you put yourself in Abbot
Nilus' care for now and let him locate a place for you to
sleep outside the walls of this holy place."

On hearing his name, Nilus steps into the cell once
again. Feardorcha nods, his eyes still lowered towards
the ground, then turns and moves in the direction of the
doorway. His movement is lethargic and uncertain, not
unlike a wild dog that has been abruptly stunned and
brought to heel. Nilus comes forward, takes the soldier by
the elbow and leads him out into the passageway.

As Benignus closes the cell door behind his unexpected
visitors, his attention is suddenly drawn to the sound of
shouting and the thunderous tramping of horses' hooves
outside in the monastery grounds. Quickly he draws up
close to the window of the cell. More of Prince Donough's
men arriving from Loughrask, he thinks at first, but then,
as he makes sense of the soldiers' shouts, he realises that
this is not the case.

"Two hundred and fifty-three of Thomond's finest
horses, courtesy of Dermot O'Brien," announces one of the
soldiers outside, and then the same man laughs heartily.

"Good work, good work," one of the Roe O'Brien
officers shouts above the din. "Get them into the enclosure
round the back."

Benignus can hear their speech quite clearly now and, as
he strains himself a little more to press his ear closer to the
conversation, one of the riders comes alongside the little
window. The horseman's presence blocks much of the

moon's light from entering the cell and casts a heavy shadow on the walls within.

"There's hardly a decent steed left within miles of the encampment at the Glen of Clab," he shouts. "By the time Dermot and his men arrive here by foot in the morning, they will be so weary from their march that they will make easy meat for our cavalry."

This time the laughter that follows is that of many men. Benignus presses his back hard against the craggy wall of his cold cell and his heart is heavy with the knowledge of what it is that is to come. He makes the Sign of the Cross, eases himself down onto the cold flagged floor and begins his nightly rosary. "*In nomine Patri et Filii et Spiritu Sancti …*"

* * *

There is turmoil amongst the troops at the Glen of Clab as Iarla moves quickly from tent to tent, rousing his father's soldiers from their sleep. Dermot himself is one of the first to emerge. He grabs his son by the arms and shakes him. "What is it, Iarla, what is it?" Iarla looks into Dermot's steel-grey eyes and he is instantly calmed by his father's stare.

"The horses, father, they are gone."

"Gone! What do you mean, boy?" retorts Dermot, smarting at the news.

"Gone, father, stolen."

Realising immediately that what Iarla is saying is true, Dermot is already pondering the implications of this disaster.

"And Fionnán, father –"

"Yes, Fionnán! Where in the name of God was he when all of this was happening?" asks Dermot angrily. "Surely to God, he could have –"

"Fionnán is dead, father, killed by the marauders," interrupts Iarla.

"Dead?" The shock and sudden whiteness in Dermot's face are obvious, despite the shadows of night all around.

"I stumbled on him amidst the bushes while bringing him a bowl of gruel. An arrowhead ate deep into his left temple."

Dermot lowers his head for several seconds, then raises it again and looks up at the moon that hangs high above the Eagle's Rock, just north of the encampment. In the distance a wolf emits a long gnarled howl that pierces the night and carries with it portents of discomfort.

"Officers," cries Dermot, as he calls the leaders of his battalions to assemble.

* * *

The echoing howl of a distant wolf reaches the ears of Brother Benignus and breaks his concentration on the rosary which he is offering for peace. Though his gift of vision has allowed him see what is to happen, he is always duty bound to surrender the realm of possibility to his Maker. Despite what has been presaged, he knows that it is never beyond the power of the Almighty to intervene and change the course of any happenings that have been prophesied.

Outside Benignus' cell and within the wider environs of the monastery grounds, things have settled for the night.

Prince Donough's soldiers have been billeted, their horses tethered and those stolen from the Glen of Clab penned within the monastery garden. Brother Germanus' monastery garden. Germanus will be less than pleased, thinks Benignus. Even Feardorcha, whose fiery temper had earlier been mysteriously quelled by the strange powers of the blind monk of Corcomroe, sleeps soundly somewhere nearby.

Benignus finishes his prayers, then, locating the little jutting stone at the level of his shoulder, he draws himself up again and stands beneath the window, facing the yellow light which the moon spills into his room. Benignus' eyes are white, as white again as they had been when earlier he had tempered Feardorcha's wrath. He fingers the centre of the same hand with which he had quietened the intruder. The flesh of his palm is sore, but he knows that, as many a time before that soreness has passed, it will also pass on this occasion. Yet again the far-off wolf emits another howl into the quiet of the night and a cruciformed shadow crosses the path of the moon, blackening the eyes of God's holy instrument.

6

Loughrask. The sun has not yet even crept above Sliabh na gCapall mountain to cast its morning light on the waters of the lake. For more than an hour past, Prince Donough and his men have been making their confessions, then busying themselves with their weapons, tightening horses' girths and then retightening them again. Père François, the French priest who some years before had come to the Roe O'Briens from their Norman allies, the de Clares, has been summoned to Donough's camp. He knows he has been called to give his blessing to the prince, just as he had done for Donough's father before he had been taken from this earthly world. Donough kneels before the priest and François rests his open hands on top of the chieftain's head. He wonders, as always he is inclined to wonder, if this may be the last time his fingers rest upon this head.

"*Oremus*," he begins in the Latin of his church, then turns to his favoured Gallic tongue. "*Je prie que le grand Dieu du ciel et de la terre te donnera le grâce et la fortitude qui soit necessaire pour gagner la victoire. In nomine Patri et Filii et Spiritu Sancti.*"

Prince Donough crosses himself as the priest completes his blessing, rises from his kneeling position, then sits and gestures to his pastor to do likewise.

"The battle, Père François. It will, I fear, be like no other battle fought in the times of the Wars of Turlough."

"I fear that you are right, my lord. It seems that this, beyond all other battles, may be the one to draw the

44

conflict to a close."

That this might well be the case was a thought which had previously entered Prince Donough's thinking. Somehow, however, hearing it spoken aloud seemed to make the possibility that much more credible than before.

"The men are restless, Père. Strange things have happened to them on this eve of battle."

"Yes, my lord."

"The elements have conspired and the men believe that Dismal of the Burren has visited herself upon them."

The priest chuckles a little, not quite enough to incur the wrath of his chieftain and yet sufficient to suggest that he is not a believer in such happenings.

"I have seen it myself, Père François, here tonight, by this very lake."

"With respect, my lord, we are called upon as Christians not to give any credence to such happenings. What we witnessed here tonight was some freak of Nature, most probably never seen before and equally likely not to be seen again."

"Hmm!" muses Donough, his tone suggesting to the priest that his explanation of what has occurred earlier in the night is somewhat different to the men's interpretation of it.

"I have spoken to the men, my lord, within the privacy of the confessional, and I have assured them that God, His sweet son Jesus and the Virgin most pure will look down upon them on the field of battle, that they will keep them safe."

"Yes. But what if they don't? What if Dismal's tidings really are to happen?"

The priest reaches over and clasps his master by the wrist.

"Faith, my lord. Faith will see all things happen as they should."

Prince Donough hangs his head. He knows his Christian belief demands of him that he surrender such things to God, but he is of a tradition which has equally acknowledged another power. He, like his cousin Dermot, with whom he will soon do battle, has been weaned on stories of the supernatural and, at times such as these, when tensions run high, it is impossible for him to be unaware of the portents that his forefathers have respected and feared.

"Fear of the Lord, that is all that is required of you, Prince Donough," François assures him.

Their eyes meet. The priest can tell that his efforts at comforting the chieftain have had minimal effect. Each realises that there is little sense in contesting these opinions. What will be will be and, all beliefs apart, they are each wise enough in the ways of the world to know that this is so.

"There is something else, Père François."

"Yes, my lord?"

"My niece."

"Ah, the lovely Lady Sorcha."

"Yes. I want you to take charge of her before the battle."

"As you wish, my lord."

"When we reach the tiny hamlet at Béalaclugga, before we make the final turn for the holy abbey at Corcomroe, I want you to take her north along the coast road to the house of the Skerretts in Finavarra. Then, come the morning, east again, then northwards to our friends the Blakes within the walled fortress of Galway."

"But if –"

"No ifs, no buts, Père François. Just tell me you will do it."

"But, my place, my lord –"

"I command you to do it!"

The forcefulness of Donough's command decides the issue and the priest realises that there is little sense in contesting the matter further. He nods his head. "Very well, my lord, whatever you may wish."

"Good," says Donough, slapping his hands down on his knees, then springing to a stand. "All that needs to be said is said and, before the sun sets over the ocean's waters on the morrow, all that needs doing will be done."

"Please God, my lord, please God."

Then both men embrace, kiss each other's cheek and move away about their business once again.

"Come on, men, get those horses into line," Donough orders, as he moves amongst his soldiers.

* * *

The rustle in the camp at the Glen of Clab has to do with anything but the readying of horses. Dermot's officers are still in shock at the news which earlier had caused them to be roused from their beds. For some hours past, alternative strategies have been discussed. So pressing is their situation that, as a new battle plan is being drafted, Fionnán's burial is being left to two young men whose duty otherwise would have been the preparation of the

horses. It is agreed that when battle has been done and
Dermot and his men head homewards once again, they
will stop on their southern journey to pay due respect to
the young man who has been taken from them. But, right
now, it is the battle that must gain ultimate attention.
Dermot is crouched low on his haunches, likewise Iarla
beside his father, and similarly the officers of the various
battalions.

"So, our sequence must be this," Dermot tells his
generals. "Archers followed by footsoldiers on the frontal
line and a combined staggered archers – footsoldiers
approach on each lateral flank."

"But, Dermot," MacNamara, one of his generals, pipes
up, "that may mean that some of our own footsoldiers on
the frontal flank get caught by the arrows of the archers on
the lateral flanks."

"I am afraid that you are right, my friend, but, given
that we are now without the benefit of cavalry, that is a risk
we are going to have to take."

"But what of those men of the cavalry?" asks a second
of Dermot's officers. "Will they now be amongst our
archers and our footsoldiers?"

"I am glad you've asked that," Dermot replies. "Some
will, some will not." And as he speaks, he places an arm on
his son's shoulder. "Iarla here will lead many of those men
as a marauding troop."

The officers look at one another. This is not a ploy the
use of which they have ever practised, though, over the
years, they have heard tales of its use by the English outlaw
Hood in the Forest of Sherwood back in the time of that
country's Crusader-king of the name of Richard – he who,

for his reported deeds of greatness, was also known as the Lion-Heart.

"Iarla," says Dermot, gesturing to his son to address those assembled.

Iarla momentarily looks at his father. He is filled with pride at being entrusted to carry out this mission. It is the first time in battle that his father has given him such weighty responsibility. He knows it is Dermot's way of beginning to hand over the reins of leadership of the clan. Iarla thinks to himself that it was probably in some such way, many years before, that his grandfather had begun to hand on his own chieftainship to Dermot. The young man shifts his gaze and looks at the officers of his father's battalions.

"Men," he says, "marauding may be a method new to us, but in it we also have the element of surprise." His speech is firm, confident, delivered in such a way that his listeners are enthused to hear what else he may have to say.

"None amongst the Roe O'Briens will ever expect us to adopt such tactics."

The confidence of his listeners is evident in their faces. Already they can see characteristics of the much loved Dermot in the young O'Brien.

"We must be swift, we must be sharp, we must be clinical in everything we do," continues Iarla. Even the style of his delivery has an impetus, his speech paced with a certainty that excites the company. "We must forget that we are without cavalry and remember instead that we now possess a weapon and a strategy of which only we ourselves have knowledge."

The officers break into conversation amongst themselves

and the approving nodding of their heads is telling of the extent to which Iarla's words are having the desired effect.

"A deadly weapon which, if used to greatest effect, can win the day for us and leave us singing on our long trek back home to the greener slopes of southern Thomond."

More talk amongst the officers and, this time, it is even louder and more indicative again of the growth in confidence that is being generated by the young leader.

"Draw closer," says Iarla, gesturing to them to come in towards him. The circle tightens and the young Iarla begins to outline his plan of action.

"This is Oughtmama, the townland east of Corcomroe, a mixture of craggy rock and scree rejected by the mountain," he begins, marking the place of which he speaks with an X in the clay. "A small advance party, not yet picked, will go before our select force. Then we will go ahead of my father's forces, cross Oughtmama east of the churches there, and continue northwards until we have passed the footslopes of Abbey Hill."

"But, my Lord Iarla, we will have gone away from the enemy at that stage," MacNamara says.

"Precisely, Fearghus," says Iarla, his confidence and his quality of leadership growing by the second, "that is exactly what is intended."

The officers look at one another, increasingly realising that they are hearing details of a strategy that is totally new to them.

"Then, brave men of Thomond, we will scale the northern face of Abbey Hill and come down its southern slope where, not only are we unexpected, but any sight of us will be lost amongst the hordes of sheep which the holy brothers of Corcomroe have grazing there."

"Excellent!" another of the officers comments. "Why would anybody think we might even dream of coming from the north when they know our camp is pitched to the south of where the battle will be fought?"

His fellow-officers' reaction to the comment suggests that they are in agreement with this observation.

"Quite so," says Iarla. "That is exactly the element of surprise we hold and, hopefully, it will prove sufficient compensation for the loss of our cavalry division."

"But what will be the nature of attack, Lord Iarla?" MacNamara asks.

"It will be simple and effective, but time enough for that when we get to the northern side of Abbey Hill. Time now is of the essence and we must march before the full light of day alerts the Roe O'Briens to what we have in mind."

"Well said, Iarla, my son," says Dermot, now taking charge of the assembly once again. "We march before the sun begins to show its signs at the back of Eagle's Rock."

The men disperse then, fired up by what it is they've heard and seeing now that what earlier they had thought to be adversity is really opportunity. Dermot draws near to Iarla.

"You have done well, my son. I am heartened that, when I'm gone, the great Clan Turlough will have a worthy leader to carry on the tradition of the O'Briens."

Father and son embrace, the younger looking over the other's shoulder to the north, where battle will be done, the older to the south where generations of O'Briens lie buried in Thomond's rich brown soil.

7

The call to break fast has just been sounded at the holy abbey of Corcomroe as Prince Donough and his men approach the monastery. The monks within the dining hall can hear the din of their arrival above Abbot Nilus' blessing of the food.

"Amen," they say in unison, the strength of their combined voices momentarily drowning out the shouting of orders outside the walls.

"It is Prince Donough and his army," Placidus whispers to Benignus as they sit in to the table.

"Yes, brother, though you seem too often to forget that it is use of my eyes that has been taken from me, not my ears."

Benignus, despite his kindly nature, is somewhat irritable. As soon as he has said this, he regrets having done so. He knows all too well how considerate Placidus has been to him throughout his years of blindness.

"Forgive me, Placidus. It is just that the night's events have done little for my mood." In fact, it is less the loss of the night's sleep which bothers Benignus than the things his gift of vision has allowed him see. And added to his gift is the loneliness it enforces on him, the need to be secretive about what is revealed to him, the pressure of deciding if and when anything that has come to him should be told.

"It is all right, Benignus, I don't think there is even one of the brethren who is at ease after last night's intrusion."

Each of the brothers then busies himself with his libum of bread and nothing is said for some minutes. Then, just as Benignus is about to speak some of his thoughts, his intention is interrupted by the noisy entry of Feardorcha into the dining hall. Again the light of the torches wedged in their cradles on the massive stone pillars is reflected in the shiny metal of the dark soldier's breastplate.

"All stand for Prince Donough of the Roe O'Brien," Feardorcha orders.

Brother Nilus is first to his feet and, very quickly, all but Benignus follow suit. His decision to stay seated has more to do with his dislike for Feardorcha than any disregard for Prince Donough. Though it is true that his natural sympathies lie far more with Dermot and his men, he has no great reason to have anything but respect for Prince Donough. Indeed, was it not Benignus himself who, some years earlier, had baptised Prince Donough's infant son before the baby died that very night of a galloping consumption. But Benignus knows the detail of the vision he has seen of late and through that he has been made all too well aware of the nature of Donough's dark lieutenant. Placidus, standing, tugs at the sleeve of his seated friend's habit.

"Stand, Benignus, stand." Placidus' urging is made in the language of semi-whisper. But Benignus gives no acknowledgement to the bidding of his friend.

"Benignus, stand. In the name of God, will you –"

"Aye, monk, in the name of God and of his lordship, Prince Donough of the O'Brien, stand," intrudes the rasping voice of Feardorcha.

Even before he has spoken, Benignus has felt the

coldness of the shadow cross his face. The old monk ignores the soldier's order and busies himself with his leavened libum. Though he cannot see the enraged expression on Feardorcha's face, he can sense the soldier's anger at him. Feardorcha raises his right hand, the pointed metal studs on the back of his leather outer glove glistening threateningly in the flaming torchlight. Once shoulder high, he makes to sweep his hand down across the old man's face. It is no more than inches from Benignus' cheek when it is seized at the wrist and stopped from inflicting injury upon the aged monk.

"No, Feardorcha." It is Prince Donough who has spoken. It is he too who has frustrated Feardorcha in his effort to strike Benignus. "What is this about? To strike a blind old man who has done no more than fail to rise at your command!"

"But, my lord –"

"Enough, Feardorcha." Prince Donough has not even looked at his man as he issues this second rebuke. Feardorcha, on the other hand, looks hard at his liege, then shifts his gaze to look even harder again at the seated monk.

"How are you, my old friend, Benignus?" Prince Donough's question is gentle and benign in tone. And now Benignus rises, reaches out and locates the extended hand of the nobleman. Once clasped, Benignus lowers his head to kiss Prince Donough's hand. Feardorcha's anger with the old man is greater than ever now, feeling, as he does, stifled by the bidding of his prince.

"Sit, please, my friend," says Donough. "All of you, brethren, please be seated." And as the brothers sit,

Prince Donough seats himself across the table from Benignus. He knows of old that the monk's allegiance lies more with his cousin Dermot than with the Roe O'Briens. But Donough, in matters of this sort, is a fair man, one who cherishes his own right to believe what he believes and similarly acknowledges the right of any other to do so also.

"You keep well these times then, Brother?"

"As well as can be expected for one of my years, my lord."

"I am glad to hear it. They are times of great difficulty for all of us."

Benignus smiles on hearing this. "Yes, my lord, as you say, times of difficulty. But, somehow, I am always inclined to feel that difficulty is as often a guest invited to the table as it is one that is visited upon us."

Feardorcha, incensed at what he perceives to be further impertinence towards his master, surges forward, again intent on dealing with the old man in the only way he knows of handling anyone who angers him.

"No," barks Donough, raising his right arm against his lieutenant's movement, "a man has right and is right to speak his mind within his place of sanctuary." He lowers his arm and leans in across the table towards Benignus. "You are a man I have always admired and liked, Brother Benignus, even though I know your heart and, I presume, your prayers to be with my cousin Dermot."

Benignus smiles. "And I have both liked and admired you too, brother Donough." He has purposely called him 'brother' rather than the more expected 'lord'. He knows that the intention in so doing will not be lost on Prince Donough and, whatsmore, that no offence will be taken by it. "But a man, my lord, who knows another's mind so well as to be able to tell him who it is that he prefers more than any other surely carries the heavy burden of great insight within him."

Now it is Prince Donough who smiles. He is all too well aware that Benignus has been touched by the Creator in a way not given to many in the earthly world.

"The gift of such insight is your's, not mine, Brother. We both know that to be the case. All I would ask is that you do not think poorly of me."

Benignus reaches across the table, intuitively locates Donough's right hand and places his own hand down upon it. The other brethren, seeing this and thinking it more forward than any should dare, are momentarily anxious at what may be the reaction of the nobleman to this gesture.

"It is not of you, Prince Donough, that I think poorly, but of this warring that has prevailed for so long. Too long! What is a Christian love if not to be at peace? And what is evil but to war? And for what, my lord, for what? Not for love of brother, cousin or kin of any kind and, most certainly, not for love of our Maker and Divine Saviour."

Donough has felt an extraordinary heat pass from the old man's hand into his own. The sensation he perceives is strange. It is both comfort and discomfort at one and the same time. Now he places his free hand down upon Benignus', spreads his fingers to clasp the edges of the monk's hand, then squeezes it a little in acknowledgement of what has been said.

"But you are a holy man, Benignus, and I a soldier and a leader of men."

"True, my lord, a leader of men. A leader decreed to be a leader by He who is the greatest of all leaders. But there are as many ways to lead as there are said to be mansions in that great leader's house, and surely, my noble lord of the Roe O'Brien, war – the killing of kinsman by kinsman, of cousin by cousin – must be the very least of these."

Feardorcha, standing all this time at Prince Donough's left shoulder, is hard put to contain himself. His dark eyes, their pupils almost as constricted as a pinpoint, have been focused sharply on Benignus as he has spoken. He cannot believe how this man has discoursed with his master, this feeble monk who has dared to place his hand upon that of one so noble, who has challenged with his turn of phrase, who has been allowed exude authority not at all in keeping with his lowly rank.

"There is but one solution, Brother Benignus, to this prolonged disagreement between the clans of the O'Brien and this very day my cousin and I will finally bring that to a close."

"Yes, Prince Donough, but on the battlefield."

Donough smiles. "But the battlefield, Benignus, is my place of work, just as your's here is the garden or the chapel."

"With respect, my lord, our places of work are those in which we choose to labour. They are not places which are blessed in themselves. It is only that which is done in such places which renders them sacred or otherwise."

Feardorcha can no longer contain himself. He cannot understand why Prince Donough has shown such tolerance towards the old man. This last comment of Benignus' has stretched his patience to breaking point again and the flow of blood to his hands seems far more rapid than that which feeds his brain. Despite having twice been previously constrained by his lord, he surges forward yet again, brushing past Prince Donough and reaching across the table to grab hold of Benignus. "Enough, monk. How dare y–"

"Hold, Feardorcha," the prince barks at him, this time forcing himself between the cleric and the soldier, and pushing the latter to the monastery floor. "There will be no desecration of this holy place and you will do well, Feardorcha, to heed my words on this."

The soldier raises himself from the floor and looks defiantly at his leader. Were he not so able a lieutenant and were the prince not so reliant on him for the strategy that would be needed in the battle, he might suffer more than a mere pushing to the floor.

"Enough," says Donough, staring down his man and causing Feardorcha to lower his gaze. The soldier winces several times in quick succession, then flinches as would an injured animal. And then he turns and storms out of the room. Donough himself now turns back towards Benignus and smiles. "I think, Brother, that you are one of very few who has the measure of my fiery officer."

"That may well be so, my lordship, but it would be better by far were he to find his own measure. Bulls thrive only for as long as they retain the good sense not to kill the cows they service." This utterance from the old man brings yet another smile to Prince Donough's lips.

"Well said, my friend, well said, indeed." Then, suddenly, Donough eases himself onto his knees before the monk and lowers his head. "I ask you that you do not, at least, refuse me your blessing on this the day of battle, Brother."

"I am duty bound to give such to you, my lordship – you know that. But it is you I bless, not the warring acts that are to come. I give it in the hope that you may yet see that there is a wiser path than that upon which you seem intent on travelling."

Donough raises his head again. "Your blessing on me then, Brother," he says, "before I leave to join my forces at the Wood of Siudaine and lead them back into this holy place before the break of day." And this time there is an imploring tone in Prince Donough's words.

Benignus steps forward and spreads his feeble hands across the chieftain's head. "*In nomine Patri et Filii et Spiritu Sancti. Pax domini magn...*"

8

Mist enshrouds the soldiers of Dermot O'Brien's scouting party as they near the rugged crag at Oughtmama, a little to the southeast of the abbey at Corcomroe. They have been led from the Glen of Clab by Cian MacClancy, a kinsman of Iarla's, and his orders are to ensure free passage for the youthful chieftain and his band of three-score select men who follow and who later hope to make their way to the northern side of Abbey Hill.

The parties have found the terrain less than kind to them, neither being used to the cragginess from which the land of Burren has taken its very name. For them the smooth lush greenness of south Thomond's gentler slopes is far more inviting. Worse still, though they do not know it, is the fact that the every move of Cian and his men has been tracked by a similar scouting party of the Roe O'Briens, sent out earlier by Feardorcha at a time when darkness had no thought of ever yielding to the light of morning. These are select troops in the ranks of Prince Donough, trained especially in the art of swoop and plunder, and totally uncompromising and merciless in their ways. Feardorcha has instructed them that, should they come on any of Dermot's men, none is to pass. "Spare nothing. Slay them as you would the briar that stands in your path or the cur that dares to cross the way of a steed when he is in gallop," were his very words to them as he oversaw the party's earlier leaving of the monastery. "And," he added, "if there is a tree from which to hang their blood-dripping bodies, then do not fail to make use of it for that very purpose."

Fortunately for Iarla and his soldiers, they have varied their itinerary from the due north course taken by Cian. The young O'Brien has veered to the northeast at that point along the route known to those who are of these lands as Bearna na Mallacht – The Gap of Curses. This will take his band of men through the hazel groves just south of Turlough Hill and, from there, into the western part of the townland of Funshin Mór. Once there, already a good one thousand paces east of Cian's projected location, he and his troops can head in relative seclusion northwestwards for Abbey Hill, hopefully avoiding all and any danger of encountering the Roe O'Brien forces. All going well, Iarla and his men will later meet up again with Cian and his party at Pluais na Leannán, the little enclave just north of Abbey Hill, known more commonly, since the coming of the Cistercian brothers to the land of Burren, as Tobar Phádraic – the well of waters, said to have been blessed by none other than Saint Patrick in his time.

Cian and his companions are nearing that point in the crag where the half-stone, half-fertile lands of Oughtmama and Coranroo pass one into the other when, unexpectedly, they hear the clanking of metal against rock not far behind them. Instinctively, all in the advance party crouch and seek the shelter of a nearby copse. Secluded in the bushes now, Cian scans the mass of moon-washed limestone out beyond the shrubbery. The landscape spreads itself in black and silver-speckled wetness. There are suggestions of shadow here and there, but none so certain as to make any of Cian's soldiers think that Feardorcha's men are anywhere as nearby as they really are.

"A goat negotiating the rock," says Cian, easing himself
into a standing position again and causing his companions
to do likewise. His announcement is followed by the
nervousness of laughter from the others and then the all
too ill-advised dissipation of that tension. Relieved at
hearing Cian's pronouncement, they turn to banter
amongst themselves when, suddenly, as does a flock of
hooded crows descend upon the carcass of an errant sheep
or goat, the Roe O'Brien scouting party sweeps mercilessly
in from all sides. The swoop is clinical and swift, so swift,
indeed, that it is difficult to discern between its onset and
its end.

Within minutes, the many acts of stab and swipe are
done and the party that was Cian and his men seems to be
no more. And before even the sharpest watching eye
among the Roe O'Brien raiders takes notice of a movement
amidst the fallen bodies, a hand stills itself a while and
waits for all to settle. It is the hand of Caltra of the Clan of
MacNamara, a boy no more than twelve summers of age,
who has travelled as a runner with the Cian MacClancy
party. He makes one of his face and the rock that lies
beneath him and none but he knows of the air that still fills
his lungs. And the only suggestion to the outer world that
anything has happened in this place is the shrieking cry of
Cian himself as an enemy dagger is driven in hard beneath
his ribcage. The cry pierces the thinness of the night air and
is carried in all directions. Its last echo, climbing well
beyond the low-set saddle of rock that makes one of
Turlough Hill and its lower limestone neighbour, Greim
Chaillí, reaches the ears of Iarla and his men.

"What was that?" asks Iarla. He stoops as he speaks, and instinctively indicates to his soldiers to do likewise. There is, however, little need for him to do so. Already they have been crouched low on the bareness of the crag, hoping that their human forms will be engulfed in the irregular shadows cast by larger rock on lesser. There is little else where they find themselves now – no trees, no bushes, not even a low-walled pen where some unknown subject of the realm might tend his goats.

"It is the night-sound of an animal, Master Iarla," says Riordan, drawing himself up closely to the young leader. His comment sounds rough and raucous, the chords that give him voice most probably raw and torn from years of roaring war cries as he has gone into battle. Iarla looks at his lieutenant in the half-light. Riordan is a man more than twice his years. He is of old Gaelic stock from Deasmhumhan, the noble kingdom of Desmond, to the south again of Thomond. His were the kinsmen who peopled the hills and valleys of every tuath in the ancient region long before the Norman Geraldines gained foothold in the place. And he has served loyally and truly on previous campaigns with Dermot and, before that again, as a noted mercenary in the armies of several others of the native kings, whether tuath or province.

It is years in Riordan's blood to stand with the O'Brien. Long spoken in his clan are the heroic deeds of his kinsman Garbhán, who, on the dark day that was Good Friday in the year of Our Lord 1014, at that place in the east where the soft lands of Cluain Tairbh stretch north from the coastal settlement of Dubhlinn, stood shoulder to shoulder with Dál Cais' mighty Brian Boru to defeat the marauding

Dane. And in his loyalty, the brave and gallant Garbhán threw himself onto a Viking sword rather than see his lord and king slain before his eyes. And such is the seed of which Riordan has been born. His years have given him a wisdom that cannot be within the gift of one so young as is his master, Iarla, and it is said of him that, like well-famed Garbhán, the only element in his make-up to surpass that very wisdom is his courage.

Iarla stares hard into Riordan's green eyes. In the night-light that is cast upon them, they are eyes that could as easily be grey or brown or black. But such is not of import beyond the fact that these are eyes that have seen far more of battle than Iarla could ever contemplate seeing. Even the scars of war that skirt Riordan's red and ragged beard, and the many more that lie unseen beneath it are testament to knowledge and experience gained.

"An animal?" the young man says.

"An animal, Master Iarla," repeats Riordan, "and only that. For if it is not an animal, then it is best that we remain not knowing what else it may be."

It is now he who stares into Iarla's eyes. A stare of firmness, stare of resolve, but not a stare in any way defiant of his leader. "Now, Abbey Hill. It is time for you to lead us on, my master. Time to be as great a leader as is your father and as was your father's father for many years before him."

Iarla's eyes hold firm on Riordan's gaze, and as they do so, a strange collage of imagery races across his mind. First, his father's face, then that of his grandfather, called up by memory of a drawn charcoal likeness he had one time seen of him, and then the smiling image of the lovely Sorcha – all people of his ken. But after these, most curiously to him, a face he does not know, a face he cannot know. It is that of a blind old man, benign and strong. The vision then is concentrated so that it is only the whiteness of the old man's eyes that now wins Iarla's attention. And in the eyes the image-within-image of a boat departing the water's edge, and hand reaching for hand – one from the parting vessel, the other from dry land.

"Time to lead, Master Iarla." It is as much the firmness of Riordan's left hand squeezing the chieftain's shoulder as the words he issues with the gesture that takes the young man from his reverie. All that has been seen within his mind's eye has happened in a small few seconds and, as Iarla focuses again on Riordan's stare, the mental image of the whiteness of the old man's eyes melts weakly into those of his loyal lieutenant.

"Time to show yourself a man true to the name O'Brien," says Riordan, and now he tightens his grip on Iarla's shoulder and gently shakes his master. Then the young man extends his own left arm and places his hand on Riordan's shoulder. "Aye, Riordan," he says, "in the name of the O'Brien."

"In the name of the O'Brien," repeats Riordan, intuitively sensing that this son of Dermot is at least – and maybe more – the man his father is.

"*Airigí a fheara*," snaps Iarla in that native way of his of drawing his men's immediate attention to him. "Single file and crouch. We make for the Corker Pass, then on to Abbey Hill." Then he pauses and looks again at his staunch lieutenant. "I will take the lead, Riordan to the rear." And as they begin to skirt the scree on the footslopes of Greim Chaillí, Riordan smiles in satisfaction.

Père François has prayed the matins in the company of the brethren in Corcomroe. Though he is strictly Benedictine, he is very much at one with the Cistercian brothers in celebrating a common Lord. Not since leaving the Abbey at Mont St. Michel in coastal Brittany to go serve de Clare, and now the Roe O'Briens, has he had the comfort of a brotherhood in making morning prayer. In most respects, life has been much easier for him in recent times and yet, something in his make-up – or, more particularly, perhaps, in his priestly training – makes him yearn for the unworldliness of monastic life again. His senses have been filled by all that he has found around him since entering the portals of this hallowed place in the dark of night. The general intrusion by Prince Donough's men has occasioned the announcement by Abbot Nilus that the brothers' rule of silence will be eased and speech is permitted between the times of matins and vespers for this day only. The brothers' attempted display of composure on hearing Nilus' decree is belied by an inner and welling sense of adventure. Their feeling is not unlike that of the excitement of the farrier's young apprentice who is told one morning that he may return home, that his master on this day will have neither wood nor reddened embers for the softening of metal, that the belly of the bellows will not again be winded until the morrow. And for the toiler, disappointment? Well, perhaps not.

Père François is fortunate that his companion at the table as the community breaks fast is the affable Benignus. Their talk in the last few minutes has been made in a peppering of Anglo-Saxon, French and Gaelic, neither man finding himself to be fully at ease in using any two of these.

An undeclared compromise has been reached and Père François' command of the Anglo-Saxon tongue, being better than his comrade's use of French, has seen the conversation being conducted in the Englishman's language. Besides, thinks Benignus to himself, François is not as old as he, so it is not unreasonable that any inconvenience should be the Frenchman's. Whatsmore, the old man somewhat uncharacteristically thinks it will, in a small way, be an experience in character-building for François to suffer the discomfort.

"It is an ugly business, this," François says. His speech is made in tempered tones that will allow his comrade hear his words, yet keep them from the ears of others.

"Yes, Père, as is any business that finds its cause in greed and the relentless pursuit of power." Benignus has been less discreet in the nature and the loudness of his comment. "It is as old as the very hills which surround us," he continues. "One has, another takes; one needs, another wants. Greed, my Gallic friend, cannot of its very nature know any lines within the realm of confinement. Its roots seek no way other than to draw incessantly and insatiably from the avaricious font of strangle-mangle."

"What you say, Brother Benignus, is undoubtedly true and yet one cannot but feel that were wisdom to prevail –"

"Wisdom, François, if you will pardon my interruption, is a commodity not common amongst those of whom we speak. Neither too is kindness, nor gentleness, nor any of those virtues that one ordinarily trusts to set the minds of fair men at odds with avarice."

The Frenchman meekly inclines his head, then smiles a smile that is more pressed than open. His gesture is as revering of the old man as it is noble, and is made in acknowledgement of the truth of all that Benignus has said.

"We are not at odds, Père François," continues Benignus. "I have my thoughts, you have your duty. Your's is by far the more weighty task, for while we both serve the Lord as common master, you, by virtue of your position, are also compelled to serve mere mortals who seem neither wheat nor chaff. Lean on your oars, my friend, and pray that the battle which lies ahead may not bear the seriousness that all the omens seem to suggest."

"But already, Brother, I have failed in my duty."

"Failed?"

"Yes, Brother. When earlier we had camped by the lake that is Loughrask, Prince Donough bound me to my duty that I should go north from Béalaclugga with his niece, the young Lady Sorcha of the Clan of Mahon, taking her this night to a safe house of the Skerretts in the area of Finavarra. Then, in the morrow's early hours, we are to proceed on to the safety of the homestead of the Norman lord, Richard le Blake of Galway."

"Well then," advises Benignus, "you must do as your master bids."

"But you yourself, Benignus, have spoken of our greater master, Our Lord Saviour Jesus Christ, and of our primacy of duty to do His will beyond all other." He looks searchingly at the stoic and pallid face of the old man, sensing that there is much going on within Benignus' mind of which he can know but less than little. "I feel," continues François, "that the larger role to which I'm called is to be with Prince Donough's soldiers as they fall in battle. What greater service to our Divine Master than to absolve the sins of His flock as these men issue their last breaths before departing the world to meet their Maker?"

"Your thoughts are noble, Père, but ill-conceived, I fear. You know already that, as we speak these very words, your earthly master is within this abbey's walls. What of the consequences should he come to know that you have not done as he has ordered? What is not known to you or any other is that which has come to me in a vision in the dark of night."

"A vision!" François' reaction is occasioned more by surprise than incredulity. Unlike the brethren at the abbey of Corcomroe, the Frenchman has no way of knowing of the gift that is sometimes blessing, sometimes curse, which the blind monk has been compelled to carry.

"Yes, François." Benignus pauses, pondering the wisdom of imparting the full detail of all that he has seen. Should he tell his comrade in religion of the young lovers' tryst which had come to him in that vision? Quickly, he decides that there is little sense in doing so. It is, he feels, sufficient that enough be said to ensure that François' decision is that he should do the bidding of Prince Donough and take young Sorcha north to the safety of the Blakes.

"There are times, *mon ami* ..." again he pauses, his endearing use of François' native tongue being much more an act of the intuitive than the calculated, "when, in this land where the pagan and the Christian worlds are at times still one, our better judgement must subjugate itself to the power of omens."

François is somewhat jolted by this latter utterance. Not so many hours earlier, by the lakeshore at Loughrask, he had occasion to react to what he perceived to be Prince Donough's over-reverence to the world of darkness. And now this from the holiest of holy men. But there is much in Benignus' demeanour that commands François' continued attention.

"My gift is not one of joy, but one of duty, my dear friend," continues Benignus. "What I see is not of my choice but of the choice of He who has given me the power of vision. It is not for me to question or reject, simply to accept that which is imparted to my blind, yet seeing eyes."

Silence. For François, it is a silence born of the necessity of time required to absorb all that he is hearing. For Benignus, it is of the wisdom of knowing that it cannot be easy for one so fervent in his faith as is the Frenchman to accommodate what is being said. It is silence's own time that tells Benignus that he should continue. The blind man faces straight ahead of him as he recommences speech.

"Dismal of the Burren is to be feared and to be heeded. And yet, she is not of this world. Similarly, in His own strange way, our Maker. Both have revealed to me in the one and selfsame vision that less than half of those who go into battle will rise and walk from the field of combat when this day is done. And of those who do survive, it would be better for them that they were even fewer still, for their greater number will carry with them marks of sword and fire that will make their lives a living hell for as ever long hereafter that they are cursed to live within their mortal states."

The pronouncement seems more issued from Benignus than his having spoken it of his own volition. And now he turns his head towards the Benedictine father. "You,

François, unless you live true to your duty and to your word, as given to Prince Donough, will be of one or other number."

The ominousness of the presage has not even fully registered with François when Benignus resumes his speech. "And even worse again, so too will be the Lady Sorcha of one or other number."

Again a silence. François' mind is doubly taxed, firstly with a coming to terms with all that Benignus has spoken, and secondly with the weight of the decision which only he can make. Time seems of little consequence to him as he tries to comb his thoughts and yet, were he outside his mind, nothing but time could possibly show itself to be of greatest import. Unbeknownst to him, his decision is made considerably more quickly than many noted men might make.

"Thank you, Benignus," he says. "All you say is right. I will take the Lady Sorcha and make north out of the kingdom of Dál Cais." And with that, he rises from the table, takes the old monk's hand, kisses it and is gone.

"God speed, Père François," says Benignus to the air, sensing that his visitor is no longer in his presence. And then the blind man conceals both hands within the sleeves of his cassock and makes to bow his head in prayer.

As the old monk nears the end of prayer, a vision cold and ugly forces itself upon his mind, interrupting this holy time which he has chosen for his Maker. At first, it is nothing more than moving shrouds of blackness across the back of his eyes. But then the image of a face which, though in his blindness he has never seen before, he intuitively knows to be that of Père François. The Benedictine's countenance is wan and agitated, his eyes as filled with fear as ever were those of any who had witnessed living evil.

And then, as though through François' own eyes, the image of a four-legged heaving mass, black and hideous, cumbersomely easing itself off of its prey. Now the seeing and unseeing eyes of the Frenchman and Benignus are as one, as they behold the dark and leering Feardorcha step aside, revealing to them the torn and ravaged Lady Sorcha. Feardorcha throws back his head in triumph and emits a cry that is of the wild.

"*Non!*" exclaims François, in disbelief at what he sees.

"No!" cries Benignus, now rising from the table at which he has been seated since the end of matins. His cry is elongated and is still issuing from his lungs as he moves quickly from the dining hall, along the arch-lined cloister and to the open door of the very cell which has been revealed to him in vision.

"Feardorcha," Benignus says, steering the whiteness of his eyes in the direction of the dark one. There is an authority that is arresting in the holy man's rebuke. A radiance issues from the monk and the soldier that is mighty dog backs away, pressing his body hard against the end wall of the cell. He is rigid, transfixed by the old man's stare.

"Père François," says Benignus, not shifting his focus of attention from Feardorcha, "take the Lady Sorcha and go, as earlier we'd discussed."

Sorcha has already eased herself up off the stone sleeping-slab on which Feardorcha had pinned her. She is shaken, her limbs and face bloodied from the struggle, her garments torn and dishevelled. And yet she has the wisdom and what little composure may be necessary to move away from Feardorcha and towards the open doorway.

"Go now, François," orders Benignus, still not shifting his attention from the Roe O'Brien lieutenant.

"But, Brother," begins François, thinking to protest the very idea that he should leave the old man alone in the company of one so dangerous.

"*Allez! Allez deux!*" barks Benignus, ending any further resistance on the Frenchman's part. His very deliberate use of François' native tongue impresses on the priest that, at this moment, there is no room for compromise in Benignus' heart. "*Immédiatement!*" the blind one rasps, driving home his desire that he should be obeyed.

François bows his head, removes his heavy cloak and spreads it across the Lady Sorcha's shoulders.

"*Mm'selle,*" he says, then escorts her gently from the darkened place, and they are gone.

A closing of the door and now there are but two. Then a sound that is more whimper than it is cry comes from the crouching figure at the end wall of the cell. Benignus knows that the power that has consumed him and is now issuing through his eyes has reduced the erstwhile tyrant to a feeble thing. The monk's face is grey and stoic, nearer in its make to marble than it is to flesh. And suddenly, a renewed surge of energy sweeps through the old man's body, concentrating its one and only escape route through his eyes. The cell is lighted as though in daytime – even brighter – and the crouched Feardorcha frenetically works his legs rat-like against the earthen floor, frantically in search of a darkened corner.

Benignus now is outside himself. Control of all that he may or may not do is long beyond him. His white unseeing eyes involuntarily focus on the ball of black that is the cowering soldier, cowering dog. And then the smell of burning. It is the smell of flesh, not anything of wood or foliage. The whimper that earlier was not even cry is now a scream. And Benignus is relentless, driven ever harder by the force that has overtaken him. Feardorcha, as though misguided in his seeking of relief from the intensity of heat, momentarily raises his head and looks towards the old man. The image is horrific. The creature's face, already almost totally devoid of features, runs as though of molten metal. And at that instant when his eyes regard the human beacon that is the monk, a further surge of energy sweeps through Benignus' frame, causing him initially to gyrate, then filling him with light from top to toe. Feardorcha screams despairingly in anticipation of what is yet to come. And just as the darkened figure braces himself in readiness for further suffering, the cell door is broken through and Abbot Nilus and two younger members of the brethren stand boldly between the jambs.

"Enough, Benignus, enough," barks Nilus, almost perfectly repeating Prince Donough's rebuke to Feardorcha earlier in the night. "I command you, brother," asserts Nilus.

And suddenly the light is gone from the blind monk's eyes, his shoulders drop and he is listless. Nilus nods to one of the fraternity who has accompanied him, indicating to him to take Benignus from the cell. And once gone, the Abbot closes the door, indicates to the remaining brother to stay back, and then approaches the huddled mound that is

Feardorcha. He crouches alongside the creature, placing the fingers of his right hand beneath his chin and raising the disfigured head to catch the strands of moonlight that creep between the window bars. He gasps at what he sees. The face is featureless and black. A mass of charred and one-time melted flesh that, incredibly, has already hardened and is set and crusted, as though it has been so for many years. Nothing but the eyes remain intact. Deep and dark and sinister. And from amidst the ugliness, they look out in their alertness and do not augur well.

"A blanket and some water, Brother, quickly," says Nilus, barely turning towards the monk who stands to the rear. The younger man turns and is just about to draw back the heavy oaken door to make his exit when his going is arrested by a noise. It is a rumbling sound from some quarter deep, that seems much more animal than human. The departing monk looks back again and there, in the very corner where only seconds earlier the seemingly defeated Feardorcha had crouched, now on all fours stands an animal much larger than a dog. It stands bold and black – blacker than the clouds of night – and seems now to have swollen to the height of any man. And its distorted face is now more obviously that of the soldier who had earlier done battle with the holy man Benignus.

Again a noise, this time much more discernedly a growl of evil and ominous foreboding, and the baring of fang-like teeth that are long and sharp and threatening. The light thrown by the moon now favours the teeth above all else, making of them something larger than they already are. The young monk, eyes forced wide in fear, makes to move away.

"Don't stir, Brother," Abbot Nilus cautions, his voice carrying in it a mixture of the knowing and unknowing. "It is better that –"

And the Abbot's words are interrupted by another growl, one more fearsome, more foreboding than before. Now, both Nilus and his comrade back away a little. Then curiously, the creature that is-and-is-not dog inclines its head in a way akin to kindness. And now a purr of sorts, far distant in its nature from the threatening sounds that have gone before it. A second purr, and the animal lowers the forepart of its body, stretches its legs to the front and rests its head upon them. No longer the baring of teeth, no longer the apparent threat. Yet another purr, and then the turning of its eyes towards Nilus. There is a kindliness in its eyes that was not there before. And the Abbot, in his wisdom, knows that if this kindliness be truth, then there is little danger. And if it be lie, then there is no greater or no lesser peril than was earlier the case.

Slowly, gently, Nilus approaches the being and, to the rear, the young monk watches. The animal purrs again, then turns in semi-submission on its side as Nilus continues his approach, and the young monk watches. Some steps on and the Abbot reaches the animal's side and it rolls onto its back, inviting the leader of the monastery to stroke its underbelly, and the young monk watches. And then, somehow, as though in a flash, the acts of approach and roll and watch seem suddenly to become as one and, in a speed that defies the capability of the human eye, the creature rolls onto its feet again, parts its jaws and snaps viciously and lethally at the Abbot's outstretched arm. The limb is caught right at the point where its lower part meets wrist and, in the very blink of an eye, the hand is severed clean from the rest of the arm and the Abbot roars his pain out to the world. Nilus writhes in agony and, in his excruciation, his screaming is unconfined. His legs are driven by a frenzy then and he moves at speed across the floor of the cell, lambasting himself hard against one stone wall and then against another, while all the time the creature, now drawn up to a height greater than any seen before, looks on … and the young monk watches.

Nilus, now at a point between two walls, stops suddenly, stands rigid in the centre of the cell for several seconds and proceeds to violently and convulsively gyrate for a time not measured. Then he stands rigid once again. And finally, after several seconds without movement, the Abbot emits a long releasing cry of pain and falls dead onto the floor. And the black creature, now drawing forward, stands over the prostrate corpse, arches its back, then paws the silver hair of the leader of this holy house in Corcomroe … and the young monk watches …

And the young monk watches. And the creature slowly turns its head, allowing its eyes find those of the fear-filled brother who now has backed against the closed door of the cell. Again the dark being inclines its head to one side, almost as though in curiousness, and the monk feels a shudder pass through his every bone and then depart his body. The creature parts its jaws, baring fangs again, and elongated talons extend themselves from the paws of its sturdy forelegs. The transformation seems more cat-like than it is canine. And in an ever-growing sense of terror, the young monk watches … the young monk waits … the young monk wilts in fear of what it is that is yet to come.

An arching of its back and the animal has drawn itself
to an even greater height, and the Cistercian brother senses
a sudden rush that is a mixture of heat and wetness coursing
down his leg. And then the pounce. Pounce and laceration.
Laceration upon many lacerations. And it is quick … and it
is vicious … and it is lethal. And now the young monk's
wait is done and he will watch no longer.

The creature backs away a little and looks for some time
at the blood-splattered wall. Then it comes forward once
again, stepping on the torn remains of its prey, and it licks
the wall. It licks voraciously, relishing the act until, in little
time at all, one would never know that this stone had ever
borne the gory evidence of what had passed just some
moments earlier. And all that had been reddened has been
rendered grey again.

The animal moves to the middle of the cell and slowly
lowers itself into a lying position midway between the
slain bodies of the monks. For a time, it licks its
outstretched forepaws, working the muscles of its tongue
hard to release the torn slivers of flesh that have remained
entrapped between its claws. It then lies over to one side
and emits a sound that is neither purr nor growl, but is
something in between. And now it stretches to full length,
forelegs and hindlimbs reaching as far away from each
other as is possible, and, as the creature does so, a change
most sinister begins to happen. Respective limbs are seen
to alter their appearance. And gradually, that which has
been animal now slowly turns into human arms and legs,
and, in that same slowness, the body that has been dog
now reassumes the form that is the dark and menacing
Feardorcha, lieutenant of Prince Donough of the Roe

O'Briens. The eyes flit from one to other corner in their sockets and only the face remains disfigured as evidence of what has happened within the confines of the cell. And now exhaustion forces sleep and those very eyes begin to close …

In a suddenness, in another quarter within the monastery walls, Benignus' eyes open. All that has passed since his eviction by Nilus has played itself most vividly in his mind. He knows already of the Abbot's fate and of that of the younger monk. Equally, he realises that Feardorcha's heart still beats strongly in his breast and that that which has passed this night is nothing to the battle yet to be fought between the elements of light and darkness. His eyelids draw themselves to closure once again, concealing all that lies behind them from the outside world.

9

The pale beginnings of another morning's sun fight hard against the early autumn mist as Iarla and his men reach the bottom of the Corker Pass. Few words have been spoken amongst the soldiers this past one thousand paces or more. The dampness of the night has thinned their spirit somewhat and even the respite offered by the solitary hour of sleep stolen hard against the rock on the northern side of Greim Chaillí seems to have done little to cheer them. The terrain has been rough and the footing most uncertain. Jagged stone has bitten at their soles since departing the Glen of Clab the previous night and, at this stage, it is only the prospect of soon reaching Tobar Phádraic that sustains the energy required to lift one foot after the other. Once there, there will be water, the opportunity to eat and, they think – not knowing of the treacherous fate already encountered by their kinsmen – to meet up with Cian and his party.

In twos and threes, Iarla's men scurry across the track at the northern end of the Corker Pass, then throw themselves into the field that will take them on to Tobar Phádraic. Only Riordan remains to make the crossing. Just as he is about to do so, a party of eight – perhaps ten – riders, escorting a half-closed wagon along the lower road that takes one eastwards towards the little fishing hamlet that is Kinvara, appears in the area just beyond Ros Sáile. They come at speed in what is neither dark nor light, but that something-in-between time that can delude the eyes. The bearded soldier crouches and waits for the travellers to pass. And then he crosses, his parting act before doing so being to look back in the direction from which they themselves have come and to scan the barren landscape for trace of any who may be in pursuit of them.

"All is clear, Master Iarla," he tells the young chieftain, as he joins his crouching comrades on the other side of the Corker Pass. "Those riders move at speed, whatever be their purpose."

"True, Riordan, but their purpose is of no concern to us," says Iarla. There is a firmness in his speech, an assuredness. But he little knows that, concealed within the half-closed wagon that has just gone the road is the Lady Sorcha and, along with her, the French priest. "Now," he says, looking towards a knuckled brow of rock that juts out from the lower slopes of Abbey Hill and from which scant smoke emits in evidence of a humble campfire, "on to Tobar Phádraic. Cian and his men are surely there ahead of us."

"Aye," says Riordan, eyeing the weakness of the smoke overhead, "but by the look of things, they'll be none too heated by the meagreness of flame." There is a chuckle from the men. "If indeed it is they who are above," cautions Riordan. "And if not there by now, Master Iarla, then we must wonder at the chance that they may come at all."

The two men look into each other's eyes. For Riordan, the utterance is born of a combination of his long experience of the world of possibility and the harsh realities of war. For Iarla, it is the mouthing by his comrade of an unannounced fear which he himself has carried in his breast the whole night long. The chieftain breaks the stare.

"Let's move," he says, and he leads the way, he and his men scything through the fern with greater ease of movement than they had enjoyed when trying to negotiate the scree on the footslopes of Greim Chaillí. They are within fifty paces of the jutting knuckle of rock when Iarla raises an arm, signalling his men to stop. "Riordan," he says.

Instinctively, the lieutenant knows what is required of him. He draws up to his master, then moves a little further ahead of him, stooping as he goes. Several paces on he stops amid the tall fern, raises his head above it, draws his cupped hands to his mouth and emits three shrill sounds that seem both hoot and whistle at the same time. And then he lowers his head again and waits. No response. He eases himself above the fern a second time, repeats the call and immediately crouches once again. Still no response. Riordan looks back at Iarla and the younger man simply nods at him, indicating to the soldier that he should try once more. The lieutenant is just about to place his hands against his mouth when, unexpectedly, there comes an answer to the previous calls. Though weaker and less confident than Riordan's efforts, there is no doubting the response. Then the puny slim figure of Caltra of the MacNamaras peeps out fearfully from atop of the rock to the front part of Tobar Phádraic and, in little more than whisper-language, he timidly asks, "Is it you, Master Iarla? Is that you, Riordan?" The boy's heart almost leaps out from his breast when, all at once, the whole of Iarla's party stand upright in the fern and roar. As soon as he had heard the voice, Riordan had instantly recognised it to be that of Caltra.

"Aye, it is, boy," he says, reassuringly. "Be easy in

yourself, Caltra. We're on the way up." And with that, Riordan looks back at Iarla and, swiftly, the chieftain and his men move towards the meeting place with an energy they had thought to be long gone from their bodies.

* * *

And to the south, others too are feeling the strains of having tramped throughout the darkened hours. Though now well clear of the wood of Coill an Áir, near to Poulaphuca, Dermot's men had found the footing amidst the density of trees there almost as difficult as had his son's party found the limestone scree on the slopes of Greim Chaillí. They are near the fork in the track known as Cabhail Sailí and already within one thousand paces of the holy abbey of the Cistercians. Wisely, Dermot had earlier decided that once this point was reached, his men would have need to rest a while. Only now are they setting out on the last and shortest leg of a journey that, in some small few hours, will find them vanquishing or vanquished.

Similarly, due north of Dermot's army, the Roe O'Brien forces trudge the final steps of a weary route to the blessed place at Corcomroe. Earlier, in the dark of night, the Wood of Siudaine – amidst whose lofty trees exactly fifty summers past, Prince Donough's great ancestor, Conor, had breathed his last breath – proved sapping of the energy of the Roe O'Brien infantry. They too had stopped a while by the harbour wall at Béalaclugga, but are now within one hundred paces of the monastery walls. The avenue leading to the abbey is lit by flaming bullrushes whose heads had earlier been steeped in oil before being mounted on the walls to either side of the approach. The light from their effusive yellow flames causes shadow to dance on shadow and wind intricately woven patterns on themselves.

"Prince Donough's men approaching. Remove the timbers from the gates," comes a cry from one of the party who had earlier arrived at the abbey with Feardorcha.

Dermot and his number, who are now themselves within five hundred paces of the turn-off for the abbey, hear the command on the thin night air. The words have carried clearly, each and every one of them as discernible to the ear as if said at no more distance than is one arm's length. Immediately, Dermot's men crouch low and scurry towards the walls to either side of the track. Then, as the realisation dawns on them that what they have heard has been spoken several hundred paces from them, they raise themselves and draw towards one another again in the centre of the roadway.

Dermot now stands at the head of his men. "*A laochra Thuadhmhumhan, a Bhrianaigh*! Warriors of Thomond, sons of the O'Brien," he says, and he moves his gaze from man to man within the gathering. And every eye beneath his stare is fixed upon the leader. "*Mórtas clainne*, pride of clan!" he continues, knowing that his words must be few, yet must be powerful, knowing that what he says must swell the heart of every clansman who stands out before him in the half-light, knowing that these very words must serve to stir and strengthen and steady for all that is to come. "The Roe O'Briens have gone on to the Cistercian abbey," continues Dermot. "There is a welcome for them within those hallowed walls that we cannot reasonably expect. The brothers there are beholden to the Roe O'Brien since before the time of Conor. But, men, let us bear in mind that we have no quarrel with our priestly brethren, nor they with us. Whatever happens from now until the time when that which is to come to pass is done, let no one of our number raise a sword or spear against any of the holy men. We are greater in deed than that and nobler and more righteous. And this is my command."

Dermot's men look at one another. There is the din of whisper now amongst their number that suggests an acceptance and a pride in what it is their leader has pronounced.

"But for now, brave sons of Thomond," recommences Dermot, "we will cross the land a little to the west and lay up a while on the northern lip of Moneen Lake. Even before leaving home, we know where lies the field of battle and, when it nears the time, we will send out two emissaries. The first north to Tobar Phádraic, informing Iarla and Riordan that we have come this far. And the second, a little later, to Prince Donough to tell him we are ready to engage his force of men."

Again, Dermot eyes his soldiers hard, fastening firm that courage in their hearts that earlier he had so eloquently mustered. "Now, mighty troops of mine," he says, "let us move as lithely as we do swiftly." And he crosses the stone divide and leads them towards the swollen lake.

* * *

To the north, Iarla and his men have gathered into the sanctuary of the roughly hewn walls of the long-abandoned oratory that encloses Tobar Phádraic. They have eaten of the food they've carried in their satchels and tasted much of the water from the holy well. But word of Cian and his men, as told to them by Caltra, has hit them hard. Apart from simple loss of numbers for the battle that is to come, even greater is the tearing at their hearts that news of the slaying of their kinsmen brings. Much is spoken of the bravery and virtue of those now gone, before the conversation comes around again to the business that lies ahead on this day of final reckoning.

"Men," says Iarla, "we will climb the holy hill to its top. From all that young Caltra here has told us, it would seem unwise to simply skirt its lower slopes to the east. It is not beyond the bounds of possibility that the very scouting party that has foully finished Cian and his soldiers still lies in wait and hopes for yet another quarry. Let us give them as little chance as would they give us."

"Amen, Amen," Iarla's men say in unison.

"Now, Riordan," says Iarla, inviting his lieutenant to come forward and gesturing to the men to widen the circle around the more generous campfire they have built on Caltra's earlier effort, "what of that which lies ahead?"

Riordan takes a stick and, out of habit, stabs the earth beneath him. Then he sweeps his feet both right and left, clearing all and any loose stone and twig that may be on the ground before him. "Here," he says, now jabbing the stick into a point in the ground with more purpose than the previous stabbing, "is where we are," and he draws a circle in the dirt. "And here, as we see above us," he continues, marking a fresh point, "is the top of Abbey Hill." He pauses to eye the gathering, making sure that they are with him in his thinking. "And beyond the downslopes to the other side lie the lands farmed daily by the brothers of the monastery. It is on these lands the battle will be fought." He moves his eyes from one to the other in the assembly. "It is on these lands the battle will be won," he says, and again he meets the gaze of many who surround him. "And it is on these lands, sons of Thomond, that the battle will be lost."

There is a travelling murmur amongst the men now. Mention of loss proves unsettling to their souls and Riordan, recognising this in them, immediately realises the need to quickly raise their spirits once again.

"If we must do battle – and we must – let us not think only fight," he says. "For if we think 'fight', let it be that we think 'fight and win'. There is no room within the breast or mind of any here to even contemplate that we might lose. We are of Thomond. And the blood of Thomond runs hot within our veins. The fire of Thomond burns hard within our bellies. We are men of mettle." And as Riordan delivers his fiery speech, his face and chest fill with belief in all he says. Young Iarla looks on in admiration. And every man present swells within himself and is filled with the same confidence and fortitude that the speaker is displaying.

"In the name of Dermot," bellows Riordan, punching the air with his fist.

"In the name of Dermot," repeat the others, and they too punch the air.

"And," says Riordan, now looking in the direction of the young chieftain of the O'Briens, "in the name of Master Iarla." And yet again he scythes the air with his mighty arm.

"In the name of Iarla," the men bellow after him and,

unknown to themselves, even the seed of thought that they might lose in battle is banished from their minds and hearts.

"Now, men," says Iarla, seeing the fire that Riordan has instilled in the bellies of his men, "let us kill the flame and gather what is our's, leaving neither sign nor breath of our ever having been here."

There is much movement within the confined space, one working his foot to and fro against the embers, so dispersing them that any sign of their light is reduced to nothing. Others cast whatever remnants of food that may lie about to the breeze that sweeps in from the nearby bay of Corranroo and then pick up the various chattels that are personal to them.

"You have done well for us, young Caltra," says Iarla, placing an arm across the youth's shoulders and raising his voice sufficiently that he brings all other business to a halt. "I ask you, men of Thomond," he continues, as he turns to face his soldiers, "has not this man of our's done well?"

"Aye!" the gathering proclaims. "Aye, he has done well."

"To Caltra!" exclaims Iarla, pumping his arm into the air as had Riordan earlier.

"To Caltra!" repeat the men, they too raising their arms and throwing their voices to the breeze with little care for secrecy. So great is the surge of pride the youth feels in his breast that his passage from boy to man has been hugely hastened by this single acclamation of the deed that he has done. To be hailed in the selfsame manner as his noble lord Dermot and Master Iarla himself had been earlier could be no small thing for one as young as Caltra.

"Riordan," says Iarla, summoning the stalwart to his side. And Riordan steps forward, carrying a sheathed weapon, and hands it to The O'Brien. Then the chieftain holds the veiled blade horizontally across both hands. "This sword and scabbard is your's, young Caltra," he says. "Wear it on your hip in memory of the bravery you have shown on this night of happenings."

Then, a simple nod of the head by Iarla to Riordan and the lieutenant steps forward once again, takes the weapon from his leader and gestures to Caltra to come towards him. The youngster does as he is bade and lifts his arm, as in time-honoured fashion, and the rugged veteran of war stoops and belts the sword and scabbard around the boy's waist. And yet again, each and every man opens his lungs to the air and bellows out a cry of jubilation.

"So done," says Iarla, "but now we look ahead. To the top of Abbey Hill, men, and there we will await news of my father's forces." And immediately, led by Riordan, they begin to move upwards against the gradient, young Caltra learning as he goes how best to hold the sword against his side so as to avoid catching it in the vegetation and doing an injury to himself.

* * *

Across the Bay of Galway, on its northern lip, and in the house of Richard le Blake, the Lady Sorcha and Père François sit dining by a huge log-burning fire. Le Blake himself stands to one side of the open hearth, sometimes conversing with his guests, sometimes quietly mulling what it is that is to be done.

"You are Benedictine, Father?" he asks of François.

"Yes, sir."

"And so, Italian too, I take it?"

"*Non, non,*" responds François, the nuance in his utterance immediately identifying his nationality to his host.

"Ah, French!" exclaims le Blake. "Well, as good fortune would have it, I have good relations with the family Llynche of this town and they, in turn, do business with the many visiting merchants from various centres in Tuscany and others of the towns as far north as the port of Genoa. You are familiar with these regions, Père?" asks le Blake.

"Only by repute, sir."

"I see. Well, what occasions me to ask is that this is what I see as the course best chosen for the Lady Sorcha, her safety, I'm sure you will agree, being of paramount importance in any decision we might make."

"Of course, my lord. As you say, of paramount importance and as in keeping with the duty placed on me by none other than Prince Donough of the O'Brien."

"Good," says le Blake, and he comes forward with enthusiasm and sits himself between Sorcha and François at the table. "This is what I think to be best," he says, spreading his hands wide on the oaken table. "The family Llynche owes me many favours and I am free to call upon them when and how I wish. In this particular matter, I know it to be within my compass to ask of them that they might arrange swift passage for yourself and Lady Sorcha to the safety of Italy. Ships carrying Italian cloth and oils are regularly in the port of Galway doing business with the Llynches. And as the tide comes in and then goes out again, so too these ships must depart this port, taking with them goods from here that are not otherwise to be had in Italy."

"Yes, sir," says François, his words inflected with a curiousness as to the detail of what it is precisely that le Blake may be suggesting.

Their host rises from the table, then moves again towards the fireplace, this time standing with his back to the lively flame. "What I propose is this, Père François: that it can be arranged that one or other of these ships, when next leaving this town's harbour wall, will take as part of its cargo your good self and the Lady Sorcha. Only those in need of knowing will be aware of this arrangement and it will be done as speedily as possible. Within the next day or two, perhaps, should things go well."

The words stir alarm in Sorcha's mind. It is as though the reality of her situation is only dawning on her now. Things have been so rushed, so handled, so fraught with danger that time has not allowed for her to think where all of this might lead. And now, for the very first time, she is mindful of the possibility that she and Iarla may be parted from each other for a considerable time and in a way that she has never contemplated. Concealed from the view of others by the tabletop, she lowers her right hand to the knotted chord where, many summers past, she had been severed from her mother and she thinks of that love which she and Iarla had made by the shoreline of Loughrask just the night before. And then the sinister shadow that is Feardorcha creeps across her mind.

10

"Man approaching from the southwest," warns Caltra, from the stone pen to which he has been posted as look-out since Iarla's party reached the top of Abbey Hill. His voice sounds firmer, much more manly than that which earlier had whispered sheepishly out into the morning hours in response to Riordan's signal. And it is Riordan now who rushes to the young man's side.

"Where, Caltra?" the seasoned soldier asks.

"There, see," the youth replies, pointing a little to the left of a cliff-face no more than three hundred paces from them. Riordan's eyes scan the landscape to the southwest. Despite there being a mist which has restricted vision since light has come, it has thinned somewhat this last short while and the soldier's gaze fairly easily picks out the moving body bobbing up and down against the greyness of the rock.

"Well sighted, Caltra, my friend," he says, slapping him on the back. "You are proving a jewel amongst men when that is what most is needed." Then Riordan leans in closer to the front wall of the pen, tightens his eyes and focuses hard on the man who bobs and weaves his way against the hill. "He is one of our's," he announces after several seconds' watching, then draws back from the wall. "Well done, Caltra, well done," he says, and again he slaps him heartily on the back. "You can hail him in when he comes within one hundred paces of us," Riordan tells him, and then the lieutenant leaves the pen and begins to make his way back towards where Iarla and the men have holed up just below the hilltop.

"Man coming in from the southwest," Riordan announces to the men as he reaches Iarla and the party. "He is one of our own."

"Most probably the emissary my father promised," suggests Iarla.

"Aye, I suspect that you are right, Master Iarla," says Riordan. "At least now we will know how Dermot and his troops are set and we can learn the whats and whens of the movements to be made."

Then Iarla and Riordan move away from the men and head back up towards the pen where Caltra awaits the messenger. As they near the post, they see that the youth has moved out to the front of it.

"Hold," the young soldier says firmly, directing his command at the man who nears the sentry box. "Hold and identify," he orders, this time issuing his instruction with an extra air of authority, and Iarla and Riordan look at each other and smile. Nothing of their thoughts is spoken between chieftain and lieutenant, but each knows that the other's smile is one of satisfaction, one of vindication of their having elevated young Caltra earlier that morning. They stand back and leave it to the sentry to see his man into the company.

Within minutes of the messenger's arrival, one of Iarla's men has burned a beart of damp twigs on top of Abbey Hill, making smoke as a signal to Dermot back at Moneen Lake and conveying the news that his emissary, Naoise, has reached them. Then Naoise apprises Iarla of the plan of action to be followed, explaining that, once Dermot has

seen the smoke, he will send out the second messenger to
Prince Donough at the monastery. The intention is, he tells
them, that battle will commence at noon on the flat land
immediately to the west of the holy place and that none
shall rest until there is a victor.

"And what of us then, Naoise?" asks Iarla. "Are we to
do as previously agreed?"

"Exactly as discussed last night in the Glen of Clab," the
messenger tells him. "And your father has instructed me
that, no matter what the circumstances that may prevail,
I am to stay with your party for the duration of the battle,
Master Iarla," he adds.

The young chieftain nods. "We will call the men together
and discuss what it is that will be done," says Iarla.

"That, of course, is necessary, Master Iarla," says
Naoise, "but would we not be wiser to await the arrival of
Cian and his men before doing so?"

"Cian and his party will not be joining us," announces
Riordan. "The evil of the night has claimed them and we
must travel lighter in our number than was originally
planned. Young Caltra out there," he says, nodding in the
direction of the stone pen, "is the only one of their band
to have survived the cut and, for that itself, we must be
thankful."

There is an awkward silence for some seconds, then
Iarla calls his men to gather in around him.

* * *

"What of our forces then, Feardorcha?" asks Prince
Donough, as he sits eating in the monastery's refectory.

"They are all but ready for the fray, my lord," the dark and helmeted lieutenant tells him. "Each chomping at the bit like the steed who wants only that the rider might ease his tightening of the reins and give him his head." There is an overly zealous and sanguinary air to Feardorcha's speech that, despite the business that is at hand, discomforts Donough somewhat.

"We do battle, Feardorcha, not because we want to but because we have to," Donough tells him. "There is less than little pleasure in this matter for me and I suspect that it is very much the same for my cousin Dermot. This is a duty which tradition forces on us, not one we would choose if it could be otherwise."

Feardorcha is hard put to conceal his impatience with this sort of speech and thinking. The animal in him can, he knows, only ever be fully gratified by the viciousness of encounter that battle-unconfined can offer. He feels the beast within him wanting to explode and can sense the flaring of his nostrils as his breathing quickens. His eyes narrow, then flit to and fro as they had done earlier when he was fully animal.

"And what of Abbot Nilus?" asks Donough. "Why has he not come to discuss the issue of the safety of his brethren before the battle rages?"

The question strikes alarm within Feardorcha's breast. As he tries hard to compose himself in readying an answer, he is conveniently interrupted by the entrance of one of Donough's servants into the refectory.

"A messenger from Dermot of the O'Brien has arrived within the monastery, my lord," the servant announces.

"Show him in," instructs Donough. And within seconds,

the emissary is brought into the eating house. He bows before Donough and then is beckoned forward by the prince.

"You bear a message from my cousin?" Donough asks.

"Yes, your lordship," says the messenger and he extracts a note from within his tunic and hands it to Prince Donough. The nobleman leans the sheet of paper towards the light of one of the flaming torches on a nearby pillar and reads.

"So be it," says Donough. "Tell my cousin that our armies will stand before each other at noon, as planned."

The messenger bows, backs away a little, then finally turns to leave. As he nears the exit of the refectory, Donough speaks again.

"And, please," he says, causing the departing emissary to turn and face him, "be so kind as to wish my cousin and his people well for me."

And, unseen by Donough, the helmeted Feardorcha sneers at what he perceives to be a weakness in his master. The messenger bows a second time and exits. Then Donough looks towards his lieutenant once again.

"So, Feardorcha, you were about to tell me of Abbot Nilus and his –"

"Brother Benignus to see you, your lordship," announces Donough's man servant, interrupting the prince in his speech. For Feardorcha, this second interruption would again be timely were it not for the fact that news of Benignus' coming to the refectory is even more of a discomfort to him than is the matter of Nilus.

"Brother Benignus!" says Donough, with that same obvious fondness for the old man that he had shown when earlier they had met, "you have changed your mind on the issue of the blessing of our efforts?" And as he speaks, Prince Donough stands and comes forward to welcome the blind monk.

"No, my lord, I fear it is not that which brings me here but something even more serious."

Already Feardorcha is seen to cower away to the side of the refectory.

"More serious, Brother! More serious than that you should agree or disagree to give your blessing to our endeavours before we go into battle?"

There is a whimper so slight from that corner of the room to which Feardorcha has taken himself that were it not for Benignus' heightened sense of hearing, it would have remained unheard by any in the world.

"It is our holy leader, Nilus," the old man tells him. And as Benignus speaks, Feardorcha is heard to rush from the refectory and down a passageway that will take him to the outer yard. Donough is momentarily distracted by the noise made by his departing lieutenant, but then turns towards the monk again.

"Abbot Nilus," says Donough. "What of him, my dear friend?"

"The head of this house is dead, my lord."

"Dead! Dead! But only earlier this night he and I had conversat–"

"Dead, my lord Prince Donough. Murdered by the one amongst your number who is in league with the darkest of all forces. Savaged by a power th–"

"Feardorcha!" interrupts Donough defeatedly, his head bowed in a sorrow that is as much part-shame in its making.

"Yes, Feardorcha," the brother confirms forlornly. "And, before that again, the Lady Sorcha."

"The Lady Sorcha!" exclaims Donough, now raising his head in great anxiety.

"No, my lord," Benignus quickly tells him, "not dead, but there are those who might think that which has befallen her to be even worse than that. He has defiled her womanhood." The baldness of the statement hits the chieftain hard.

Again, Donough lowers his head and sighs.

"She had been here unknown to you, but now she is gone in haste to safety along with the French priest, as you had earlier commanded."

Slowly, Prince Donough raises his head for a second time, his face now red and contorted by the anger which he is striving hard to contain within himself. His lungs fill, his chest swells, he is a man at once at odds with himself that he has not taken steps before now to restrict the bloodthirstiness of his dark underling.

"Feardorcha!" he roars with all his might and anger, the word reverberating throughout the refectory as it bounces off one wall and then against another. And the sound of horses' hooves is heard galloping from the yard outside.

"Too late, my lord," says Benignus calmly. "He will do what he will do and there is only one who has the power to quell him."

Donough looks at the monk, knowing, despite the obvious frailty of the old man who stands there before him, that it is only Benignus himself who has the wherewithal to confront Feardorcha.

"It will be done when it is done, my lord, but nothing

now can stop the battle that is to come."

Donough looks curiously at the wise man. There is, he thinks, a resignation in his speech which, to him, seems strangely at odds with the monk's more usual certainty and composure.

"Please kneel, my lord," Benignus says, extending his arms invitingly, his palms turned upwards as a sign of peace. Donough falls to his knees, blesses himself with the Sign of the Cross and again bows his head. "For a second time within a small few hours, and as one who calls you friend, I give you my blessing, Prince Donough, but I cannot bless the deeds that may happen on this day. As a humble monk of peace, it is not within my gift to assist in any warring effort, regardless of it culminating in victory or defeat." The blind one pauses momentarily. "I have seen it at the back of my eyes," the old man tells him, "that today there will be no victor. There will be only those who lose." Benignus places his hands on the chieftain's head, prays his blessing on him again and steps back.

Then the chieftain rises. In a strange way, his greatest feeling in Benignus' presence is nothing if not one of extreme humility. "I thank you, Brother," he says, "I thank you even if your blessing cannot extend itself beyond me." And Benignus makes what is almost a non-discernible inclination of the head in acknowledgement to him.

"Please, Brother," he says, taking Benignus by the arm, "come sit and speak with me a while," and he leads the monk to the bench that is opposite where he himself has been eating at the dining table.

* * *

To the north, in distant Galway, the Lady Sorcha and Père François have risen after some small few hours' sleep and are again seated opposite each other at the dining table in the house of Richard le Blake. Only seconds earlier they have heard the sharp clip of shodden hooves hard against the cobbles of the courtyard outside. Then the heavy oaken door into the room opens and le Blake sweeps in with gusto.

"Good news, my friends, good news," he proclaims enthusiastically, and he lobs his hefty frame onto another of the chairs at the table. "The family Llynche, I have spoken to them and, as I had suggested earlier would be the case, they are more than happy to oblige me in this business." Sorcha and the priest look at each other, he with a mixture of delight and relief, and she with nothing other than a sadness. Her greatest thought and deepest fear are one – that she might never in this world again see the eyes or feel the warmth of young Iarla. She is as speechless in herself as is le Blake delighted.

"I can tell, " le Blake says, with an air that is tinged with more than a little pomposity, "that I have taken you aback with the speed with which I have managed to confirm this arrangement, but let us simply say that power carries with it its own package of privileges." Sorcha almost resents the element of self-adulation in this pronouncement, but she knows that her perception in the matter is all too heavily weighted by the depth of sadness in her heart.

"Now, Père, my Lady Sorcha," says le Blake, rising once again and moving towards the fire that still burns brightly in the grate, "let me apprise you more fully of the necessary detail in relation to your imminent departure from these shores."

Le Blake pauses in considered measure, strides two or three times across the face of the hearth and then proceeds. "The ship is the *Bella Donna*. She is out of the port of Genoa and she sails under the stewardship of the Venetian, Giacamo Annelli, captain of the vessel."

Even these first few details register hard and bitter in Sorcha's young heart. She is at pains to grasp the reality of what it is that is happening here. It is as though all of this has come about far too quickly for her. Less than one full day earlier, she had seen her lover in the seclusion of the woods below Killoghill and there was nothing in the world for her but him. Now, suddenly, she is to be whisked away from him and from everything she knows and cares for, and lodged in some foreign land, perhaps never even to see her Iarla again.

Le Blake is oblivious to any sense of distraction which Sorcha may be feeling. There is, of course, no way that he could know of the tearing that the young woman is feeling in her heart. He is strident now in his delivery of the details and boosted in himself at his success in having called in the favour owed him by the Llynches. And, perhaps more tellingly, he is aware that having obliged Prince Donough in this deed, and so too, indirectly, the Norman lord de Clare, he himself may gain further favour.

"The *Bella Donna*," continues le Blake, "leaves the port of Galway at the hour of midnight this very day. She carries with her skins and rolls of woollen cloth destined for the town of Lucca in the region known as Tuscany." He looks a moment at Père François. "You have, no doubt, heard of Tuscany, Père?" he asks.

"But, of course," François replies, in that very French

way that again marks him out as being of no other nation.

"So," continues their host, "once on dry land, it has been arranged that Captain Annelli will put you in the care of those who will take the goods from dock and on to Lucca. There you will stay a short while with the trader, Salvatori Rossi – he is, I am assured, a good man and honest in his dealings. And then, after a number of days have passed, you will be taken by wagon to the safety of the Benedictine holy house at Monte Cassino."

"Monte Cassino!" exclaims François. It is amazing to him that out of such adversity should come the opportunity to see the holy place where Benedict had so long ago founded the very Order to which he now belongs and to whose ideals he has committed his entire existence.

"*Exactement*, Père," says le Blake, with an attempted Gallic flourish. He is revelling in the role of being the harbinger of what he believes to be such good news. But, as the priest's spirits are elevated by what he hears, Sorcha's heart grows heavier by the second. Lucca, Monte Cassino or any other such exotic places are much too far away from where she would rather be.

11

The mist has thickened over Abbey Hill and a biting cold has crept into the morning. And further south, on the very field in which the battle is to be fought, it is even gloomier again. The land there is akin to an earthen saucer that, in weather such as this, entraps whatever conditions that prevail and is always last to let them go. Visibility for the fight will not be good and even worse again is Iarla's anxiety at the futility of trying to signal his father by smoke, informing him that they are ready to march and join with him. Iarla and Riordan have moved away a little from the men and are seated on a boulder from which, in fairer circumstances, they might see the lushness of the monastery's rich farmland in the distance.

"It is not good, Riordan," Iarla remarks.

"No, not good, Master Iarla, and if I am a judge of anything in matters of this kind, it will not be getting any better. There will be days of this before a blueness visits itself upon the skies again."

"What do you advise, comrade?" And as Iarla seeks the counsel of his loyal lieutenant, he places the hand of trust upon Riordan's shoulder.

"Advise!" says Riordan. "I am near afraid to suggest anything, but advising nothing is little more than to accept defeat before a sword is even wielded." Then the officer is silent for a time and he gazes at the thickness of the mist as it envelops them. Iarla watches as Riordan's eyes scan the nothingness before them and the lines worn deep into the lieutenant's forehead furrow as he contemplates the situation. And then, almost as if to clear his mind of any thought that might stand in the path of reasoned decision, he rubs his forehead with his hand, banishing the lines that had seemed to claim it as their own.

"Two things, Master Iarla," he says. "One is that we march as planned. There is no sense in taking any other course. The battle will happen on this day with or without us, and so the decision is made for us on that question."

Iarla watches the resolve in Riordan's face as he speaks. His decisiveness is testament to years of service, years of wisdom, years of making the hard calls when that has been what was needed.

"And the second?" invites Iarla.

"The second is that we disobey your father's instruction about keeping Naoise with our number."

"Disobey!" exclaims Iarla, flinching at the very suggestion and removing his hand from where it rested on the soldier's shoulder. He is taken aback somewhat that such should come from one so loyal as is Riordan.

"There is this, Master Iarla," says Riordan, quickly sensing the nature of the young man's reaction and intent on assuring him that this decision has to do with anything but disloyalty on his part. "Firstly, because of the mist, we cannot communicate with your father by smoke. In the second place, we move by foot and so do not even have a horse on which to send a rider to him. But if we fail to contact him by some means or other, all things are thrown into confusion and it is certain that we will be vanquished by the greater forces of Prince Donough."

Riordan's paced and measured delivery impresses itself

on the young chieftain. After all, thinks Iarla, was it not the need for clarity of vision and decisiveness that occasioned him to seek the lieutenant's advice on the matter in the first place. The younger man nods. "You are right, Riordan, my friend," he says. "You are right, as ever is the case. We will do as you suggest. Naoise will be sent and all confusion will be avoided. I am grateful to you for your wisdom." And as he speaks, Iarla places his hand firmly on the soldier's forearm.

But doubly impressed by all of this is Riordan. Not for the first time in a small few hours has he been witness to this young leader's own decisiveness. It warms his heart much to know that whatever be the outcome of the fray that lies ahead, the future of the Clan of Dermot, the O'Brien, will, it seems, rest in the safest of hands for however long young Iarla breathes breath within his lungs. Riordan places his free hand down upon that of Iarla.

"There is an even greater wisdom than a body's ability to give advice, young Master Iarla, and that is one's ability to take advice. And you are amply blessed in that respect." Then Iarla caps their regard for each other by placing his second hand on Riordan's, and they are firm and strong and fully given to all that is to come.

"And now, Riordan, if I may, I would like to take a little time alone to think on matters," says Iarla, breaking the link between them that is hand on hand. "Much has happened and it has happened in all too short a span of time. There has been but little chance for me to make sense of it in a way that I would like."

"Of course, my friend," says Riordan, rising, knowing that his use of the term of amicability is not too daring and is a further sign of the bond of comradeship that has grown between them. "I will see to dispatching Naoise on the errand on your behalf, should you so wish."

"That would be good, my friend," says Iarla, deliberately confirming the tie between them by using the selfsame word of cordiality as had his comrade only seconds earlier. Then Riordan is gone and the young man is alone.

There is nothing but the mist. The only thoughts to visit Iarla's mind now, as he sits upon the massive limestone rock, are those of the lovely Sorcha. So many things have happened and all too quickly, as he had intimated to Riordan. Throughout the arduous night that has passed, he has had to force himself not to dwell on thoughts of her. When there was the possibility of danger as they crossed the rock, it was on that danger he had concentrated. When there was need to make decision, that was where his mind was placed. His has been the role of soldier, the role of leader, and needs must that matters of love would be of another time.

But now he takes that time. He has no knowledge of what may lie ahead for Sorcha, neither has he notion of what the future holds for him. As far as Iarla knows, his loved one is now safely with her cousins back in Muckinish. He is totally unaware of Prince Donough's prior arrangement with Père François, that the priest should take her north to Galway, and he is equally as ignorant of the imminence of her departure to places he has never dreamed of – indeed, never even heard of. Had he but whisper of her leaving, then that escorted wagon from which they had earlier rushed to hide themselves at the bottom of the Corker Pass would not have gone the road unhindered. But no. Now, his singular resolve is that he will survive the carnage that he knows must come. Survive it for no greater reason than that he will be with his Sorcha at last. And she with him. And deep within his heart, there is the dream – the hope – that their union in the future may be the cause of peace between the warring O'Brien factions.

Here now, as he thinks of Sorcha, little and all that he knows of her leaving on this very night, he is even less aware of that which has passed between herself and Feardorcha. And, indeed, if he were to know, how poorly might that serve in the day's battle? Were he to meet the dark one on the field in the knowledge that the Roe O'Brien soldier had defiled his treasured Sorcha's honour, how then would be his judgement? Might not anger be his greater part, compromising him, rendering him more vulnerable to injury than would be the case were he to be more collected? This way his head is clear, despite his heart being torn. And so, first things first, he thinks, and when all is done there will be time for love, time for Sorcha.

Iarla looks hard at the mist that enshrouds him. Such now is its density that it is difficult for him to discern any distance between it and his face. It is as though he somehow belongs within it, nestled in its murkiness. And suddenly, in that very darkness, coming towards him, the young O'Brien sees what at first he thinks to be a light. Then, it seems to him that it is not one light, but two. Yes, very definitely two. And as they near him, there comes with them a warmth that quickly eases any feeling of anxiety that may be rising in the young man's heart. So entranced is he that he is totally oblivious to Naoise's going by him as he leaves on his way south with news to Dermot.

12

It is only the relative brightness at a particular point in the sky, as the sun still tries in vain to defeat the mist, that lets Iarla and his men know that the noontime is little more than an hour away. They move carefully, curiously finding the footing on the southern downward slope of Abbey Hill even more precarious than when earlier they had moved against the gradient of the northern face. An errant stepping on the looseness of the scree that peppers the ridges they traverse in their descent could all too easily relegate any of their number to the bottom of a cliff-face. Several times already, as they've moved from ledge to ledge, they have come upon the flesh-picked heads and broken ribcages of animals who have met that very fate.

Once at the foot of Abbey Hill, though still on rock, Iarla decides that, given the uncertainty of the terrain, it is best for them to make for the fertile fields known locally as Abbey East. This way, at least, though drawing them somewhat nearer to Prince Donough's forces than they might otherwise desire at this stage, there is less of a danger that they will be tired out by the demands of crossing the unforgiving stone. Anyway, Iarla's decision, like all that he has made before it, is measured and assured. His men's well-being must, at all times, be paramount in his thinking and he knows many of their number to be sufficiently seasoned in the ways of battle to realise that, in lands as open as are these which they now enter, one moves swiftly, keeping the head low and the body as bent and near the ground as is ever possible.

In little time at all, they come to an enclosure made in stone. Though vacant, its proximity to the monastery leads them to think that it is, most probably, a pen for animals used by the monks. Once inside, they rest a while against the walls, temporarily divesting themselves of the weight of weaponry and satchels which they carry. They are almost at a point where, were their circumstances different, they might allow the period of respite pass into one of comfort when, unexpectedly, they are jolted by a shout.

"Look! Look, Master Iarla," cries Caltra, excitedly. He has wandered outside the pen and is pointing in the direction of a solitary wind-bent tree that stands no more than fifteen paces beyond the enclosure. Immediately, the men within the pen are on their feet again and both Iarla and Riordan at once draw up against the inner side of the dividing wall as they watch the boy draw closer to the form that he has pointed out to them. They screw their eyes hard against the mist as they look to where young Caltra points and slowly, surely, they begin to make some sense of what it is they see hanging from one of the lower branches of the tree.

"It is Naoise," Caltra says, looking at the blood-drained body that dangles lifelessly above his head. "He has not made it back to Dermot's camp."

"Naoise!" exclaims Iarla, as first he looks at Riordan, then shifts his attention again to the young soldier still outside the pen. "Get back in here, Caltra," he orders. The youth, as though in shock, seems strangely caught between the worlds of knowing and not-knowing. He looks back at first at Iarla, then raises his eyes again to view the suspended corpse, little knowing how horrible a sight it really would present were he to see it in better light.

"Now!" barks Iarla, his voice this time imbued with a mixture of anger at not being immediately obeyed and an intuitive perception of the imminence of impending danger that may lie ahead. The curtness of Iarla's command registers with Caltra and the young man backs away a little from the hanging Naoise. Then, sensing something of that danger to which his master is already very much alerted, he turns and makes hastily back towards the relative safety of the pen.

Once inside the stone enclosure, Caltra seems eminently more aware of danger being at hand. It is as though his reaction to that which he has seen has been delayed and he is only now beginning to make full sense of it. Suddenly, he is breathing rapidly, almost uncontrollably. He slumps down against the hardness of the wall, pressing his back firmly to the rock.

"Easy, *a mhac*, easy," Riordan tells him, as he comes towards the youngster. Then he stands over Caltra and lowers his hand down onto the boy's head. "Easy," he says again, as would a rider to a troubled steed. "Breathe steadily and slowly, lad," he tells him, now bending low on his haunches alongside the youth. And gradually Caltra begins to regain a little of his composure.

"Riordan," comes a call from outside the pen. It is the voice of Iarla. The lieutenant stands and sees across the wall that his young master has made his way out to where Naoise's body hangs. "A word with you, please," says Iarla.

"Aye, Master," responds Riordan, and he stoops again

for a moment beside Caltra. "Take your time, son," he tells the boy. "Slow and easy breathing, lad, and I'll be back with you in no time." Then he rises once again and makes towards the chieftain.

Iarla's gaze is lowered towards the ground as his lieutenant reaches him.

"Look carefully at him, Riordan," says Iarla. "Look at his arms."

The battle-hardened officer draws closer to the suspended Naoise. All he has encountered in years of fighting fierce campaigns has inured him to the worst of things and there is little left that can move him in a way that might touch a lesser man. His gaze now is focused on Naoise's arms, just as Iarla had directed, and, as his eyes and mind combine to make sense of that which is to be seen, he flinches and then recoils in horror. His immediate reaction is to cup his hand against his mouth to contain the vomit he feels rising from his innards. But, even then, the strands of food-laden bile make their way in green and brown from out between his fingers. He turns away and empties his belly to the world. And Iarla now is at his side.

"What has done this to him is surely not of animal or human kind," says Iarla.

Riordan turns again to view the body. He winces as he again takes stock of the torn serrated flesh that hangs loosely from the upper arms on either side. And below the point on each limb where there would be elbow, there is nothing to be seen. Again he feels a momentary convulsion rising in his stomach, but this time he contains it better than before.

"There is but one creature I can think of who is capable

of barbarism of this nature," says Riordan, his eyes filled with terror as he looks at Iarla. "And that creature is both beast and man, and yet never fully either."

Iarla's eyes widen. "Feardorcha!" he says.

"None other, Master Iarla."

And both men turn their eyes to regard the lofty monastery, first ever founded as a place of peace, a place devoted to all that should be good.

* * *

"Roast them, slice them, cut them down with every turn of blade, men. For if you fail to do so, you will have me to answer to," bellows Feardorcha at his assembled troops, as he paces back and forth across the cloistered quadrangle of the monastery. And every eye is fixed on him in his strident movement. Huge yellow flames dance violently beneath a massive cauldron of boiling oil, which sits mounted on a wheeled wooden frame in the middle of the open space. Both cauldron and frame seem held within a catapult-like harness to the sides of which a taut and woven straw rope is attached. This serves as a retaining band, so that, in the event of movement, the gigantic pot will not be toppled over. Yet, were the restraining rope to be cut, the cauldron would be jettisoned forward and its contents spilled without confinement. And in their dance, the brightness of the flames beneath reflect themselves in the blue-black metal of the dark one's breastplate. Nothing of his person is to be seen other than the black and piercing eyes that look out through the open visor-gate of his helmet.

"These are vermin, scum, lower than the lowest that

your minds can call to consciousness, and you must deal with them accordingly," Feardorcha continues. And now he stops his pacing and eyes the gathering squarely. "Spare nothing," he commands, "give nothing, treat them with the ruthlessness deserved of any of their kind that might ever dare to creep out from beneath a rock."

His men respond to his exhortation with what seems a sinister mix of grunt and chant.

"When your swords are held aloft in the fever of the day, let whatever light there be catch nothing but the sight of blood and gore as they run down your weapons' blades from tip to hilt," continues Feardorcha, deliberately manipulating his listeners' minds and working them towards a greater frenzy.

And this time his men's response seems even more primeval than before. It is near-animal in nature. Feardorcha swells with a conceited pride in the knowledge that every man before him is fully in his grasp.

"Tear out their hearts, cut out their eyes. I want limbs and heads and every body part strewn across the field of battle so that it is known to all and sundry everafter that there is a cost to be paid by any who dares to stand against me."

Again, the same disturbing reaction as before is issued by his listeners and, as the frenzy amongst his men seems to serve itself, Prince Donough, somewhat concealed from view, draws up against one of the limestone columns in the cloistered walkway. His face is owned by worry's shadows. He knows that all control he has ever had over his own soldiers has finally passed from him and that they are now fully in the grip of another prince – this prince of darkness

– that is the ever-swelling, ever-fearsome Feardorcha.

But that inner honour that is Prince Donough's – an honour common to the men of the Clan O'Brien, no matter what their hue – mounts in the nobleman's breast and, despite his sense of helplessness in the situation that is at hand, he knows he cannot allow that which is happening to pass without his interjection. He feels his protest rising from deep within his soul and is at a point where now it is independent of his will and cannot be halted, regardless of what he may or may not do. An hysteria amongst the troops, generated by Feardorcha's masterly and calculated stirring of their emotions, is at fever-pitch when Donough intervenes.

"No!" he shouts, the single word of resistance drowning the hubbub of the frenzied mob before him and causing each and every head to turn in silence and regard him where he stands. As if delayed by some strange trick of nature, the short and solitary word reverberates throughout the quadrangle, seeming somehow to bounce itself from wall to wall within the cloistered area. And Donough feels the eyes of every man upon him, feels the eyes of every man against him, feels, above all else, the eyes of the unrestrained and crazed Feardorcha burning hard into his very being. And then a silence. It is a silence that is as intense as it is long.

"Ta-a-a-a-ake him," bellows Feardorcha, his order to the men elongated in speech and shrewdly delivered so as not to lose the momentum of all that's gone before.

And as quickly as is Feardorcha's command issued from his mouth, Benignus is at Prince Donough's side and, alongside the monk, stands the same servant who earlier, in the small hours of the morning, had announced Benignus' desire to speak again with the nobleman.

"Quickly, my lord, you must go," Benignus says, and before the blind and seeing eyes can meet each other, Donough is whisked away at speed by his servant.

"Ta-a-a-ake h-i-i-im," comes Feardorcha's instruction for a second time. But already Donough is gone and heading for a secluded cell within the walls where he will be locked away from harm. And now, from that point where earlier the leader of one half of the Clan O'Brien had stood and made his protest, the ever-staunch Benignus steps out into the light. His eyes are bright and radiant, and none knows better than the onlooking Feardorcha just what the power of those whitened orbs can be.

"Hold!" barks the renegade lieutenant, instantly quelling the bloodlust he has generated in his troops. He can feel his heart race against itself within his ribcage. His nostrils flare, just as they have done at other times of anger. He contains himself, allowing the flow of greatest heatedness to pass. "Hold, men," he instructs again, and this time it is said somewhat less abruptly than before. And the instrument of darkness looks hard at his adversary for several seconds. The monk holds his head high. A white light, stronger than the power of any stare, emanates from his eyes. Then, picking his own time, Benignus slowly turns and calmly feels his way down along the colonnaded cloister, finally disappearing from the view of the onlooking soldiers as he enters a doorway that will lead him back into the bowels of the monastery. And in relief of sorts, Feardorcha exhales long and hard, driving shafts of vapour out against the murky dampness of the lurking autumn air.

His nemesis is gone for now.

Slowly, Feardorcha's eyes scan the troops before him. They are still fully in his grasp, none of their number knowing anything of how the old blind monk had earlier reduced their evil leader to a feeble cowering figure. He realises now that Prince Donough is out of the frame and that this day of days can be his alone, if all goes to plan. Equally, he knows, he must keep his men at evil's edge until all that is to be done has been completed.

"Kill," he says, softly. "Kill," and this time it is said somewhat more harshly. "Kill," he says a third time, all semblance of gentleness banished from the utterance now. And already the repetitious murmur is mounting amongst the men before him.

"Kill," comes the mob response, initially with something of the softness with which Feardorcha had first delivered the same word. But, very quickly, the communal mind finds the harshness that the leader has intended and, in no time at all, the growing chant takes on the viciousness Feardorcha has desired. And now, each time that the single word is issued, the soldiers pump their weapons hard and high into the air, and the noise that's made is almost mantra-like and is that of shout running into ever-frenzied shout. "Kill-kill-kill-kill-kill …"

* * *

Sound carries unevenly in the dampness of the air and, within the distant enclosure, Riordan has cocked his ear for fully one half minute before interpreting what it is he hears.

"Master Iarla," he says, beckoning the young man

towards him. Iarla comes quickly and Riordan takes him by the arm and leads him out of the enclosure once again and back towards the mountain. Then they both crouch down beside each other. "Listen," invites the older man, pointing towards the abbey. And Iarla concentrates his mind on what it is he's hearing and, within seconds, he too interprets that which is being chanted.

"It is getting nigh, Master," says Riordan. "Men cannot be worked this way and then let off the heat. Even lesser warriors than yon Feardorcha know that much. He is working them to fever-pitch and he is well aware, as are you and I, that that cannot be done a second time."

"What you say is right, my friend," says Iarla. "But what are we to –"

"Master Iarla, Master Iarla," comes a cry from Caltra, interrupting the young chieftain's speech. The boy has stood at that spot against the enclosure's wall where earlier he had slumped and he is looking to the west of where they are. "Prince Dermot," he shouts. "Prince Dermot and his men approach."

They look beyond the pen, but can see nothing in the mist.

"It is Caltra," observes Riordan. "He is raving with the shock of what he has seen earlier. Come, Iarla," he says, again taking his young master by the arm and running with him back towards the walled area. But, as they near the pen, the density of mist is thinned by their being closer and the evidence of their own eyes quickly tells them that young Caltra is anything but raving. Coming towards them, across the field on which battle will be done, they see the ordered marching lines of Dermot and his men. And Iarla and his loyal lieutenant go further out across the field to meet their brothers-in-arms.

13

There is much bluster and scurrying about the house of le Blake in Galway. Servants, male and female, have been toing and froing since mid-morning, readying trunks of clothing for the Lady Sorcha to take with her on her journey. Madame le Blake and her daughter, Veronique, are near enough of a size with Sorcha and their parting with several of their dresses and other items of their wardrobes in the young lady's cause is as self-suiting an act as it is one of philanthropy. As many of their standing amongst the gentry of the town of Galway know, such acts of apparent generosity merely create a convenient excuse for noble-women such as they to replenish their stores of finery. It is a perfect opportunity for the women of this house to replace these cast-offs with newer garments, those made of the very best of Italian silks and laces, or of satins most recently arrived on these shores from the eastern port of Tseutung in far off Cathay.

"It is nearing a quarter past the hour of eleven, Lady Sorcha," says Madame le Blake. "Will you dine with us below in another half-hour's time?"

Both questioner and speech impinge upon the privacy of thought that has filled Sorcha's mind for some time past.

"Yes, Madame le Blake. Thank you very much," says the mildly startled young woman, while, at the same time, she lifts her legs from the deeply set window-seat at the gable end of the bedroom where she has been resting since earlier in the morning. She looks towards the affable lady of the house standing in the doorway. She is elegant – tall and slender – and bears all the signs of having fought the test of years quite well.

"One quarter of the hour to twelve then, Madame."

"One quarter of the hour," repeats the hostess, and she is gone as quickly as she had entered Sorcha's thoughts.

Sorcha's thoughts: they are in major part, of course, thoughts of Iarla – thoughts of where and how he is and if, perhaps, by some unforeseen intervention by Fate in the scheme of life, the day's battle is not to happen after all. And things will be miraculously peaceful and harmony will prevail far into the future. But even Sorcha, tender though she be in years, is realistic enough to know that this is not the way that such matters come to pass. She is of a family that has seen the ugliness of war in its every generation. Indeed, though thoughts of Iarla fill the larger corner of her mind, she is not heedless of the fact that her own father, Mahon, will stand with the opposing forces of the divide on this day's fighting. And many cousins too, on either side, will fight and fall, or even try to flee the frenzied heat of the foray.

The le Blakes have been kind to her since her arrival in their dwelling, the women of the house being most attentive, yet at the same time unobtrusive. As for le Blake himself, his way of kindness is best seen in his pragmatism. He is the doer of things and has particularly enjoyed being seen to be acting in this matter. There is no telling how his day – and, even more so, his sense of self-importance – has been lifted by his going to the dockside to arrange the necessary and by his ability to call in one or other of the many favours that have been due to him for some time past. Such command of things is, in his estimation, the essence of what rank and privilege is all about.

But Sorcha's mind also harbours thoughts of greater darkness, thoughts which she wishes above all else she could speak of to an intimate and understanding listener. And now she turns her thinking to her fears. Though the le Blake women could not have been kinder to her than they already have been, she knows neither of them sufficiently well as to dare begin to tell of how Feardorcha's violation of her person has affected her. Dark and haunting shadows pass themselves across her mind with increasing regularity and the thoughts of the defilement which has been done to her increase her awareness of the physical soreness she is sensing. She can feel the pain of bruising on her body and a burning rawness of flesh where she has been torn. And even worse than this is the fear – the most dread-filled possibility – that, already, she may be with child. And if so, despite her intimacy with Iarla, she may never know whether the seed that may be growing deep within her is that of her cherished lover or the poisonous Feardorcha.

The sound of the great brass dinner gong in the hallway of the house jolts Sorcha's mind from the business of its musing. So heavy have been her thoughts that she has had no sense of the passage of time since Lady le Blake had looked in on her. She gathers herself, straightens her attire, assiduously brushes an imaginary something from the bodice of her dress, then makes for the company below.

* * *

Orders being barked, the clanking of metal against metal and the sound of crunching feet grinding hard against the gravel in the monastery's outer yard fill the air. The boiling cauldron has been rolled out to the main gate and a huge forged-iron lid has been bolted down on it, preventing any spillage that might otherwise be occasioned by the movement that will lie ahead. Then a team of heavy, toil-hung horses is hitched to the front part of the wooden frame on which the massive container is still mounted. And all this time the flames dance on the iron plate beneath the pot's big belly and will continue to do so when the cauldron of bubbling viscous liquid is drawn onto the field where the battle will be fought. And overseeing it all, dressed fully for the fray, Feardorcha sits upright on a stallion that is as black of coat as are its rider's eyes.

Unseen even by the wily gaze of the evil one, Brother Benignus exits from the body of the monastery and makes his way down along the cloister. As he reaches the penultimate arch, he disappears from view and re-enters the building at that very point where, earlier, Prince Donough had been ushered hastily to safety. Once inside, Benignus' senses are keener than are those of even the most seeing of beings. He feels his way along the wall of an inner passageway, then down some steps, eventually finding himself at the doorway of a stone cell.

"My Lord Donough," he says in whisper, drawing his mouth up closely to the barred opening in the upper part of the broad oak door. "My Lord Donough," he says again, "it is I, the monk Benignus."

"Benignus!" exclaims Donough, moving desperately towards the opening and pressing his face hard against the bars. "What news without, my friend?"

"They are readying to make for battle, my lord."

"Make for battle! Without me, Benignus? How can they march to war without their leader?"

"Their leader has declared himself, my lord, and, whether out of fear or for some other reason, they have chosen to give their loyalty to him."

"Loyalty! To Feardorcha?"

"Yes, my lord."

"But he is not of good, my friend."

"Not only not of Good, my lord, but most decidedly of Evil."

Their speech is the whisper-language of secrecy that is so frequently invited to the world by some sinister combination that is the product of darkness and uncertainty. The prince of one half of the Clan O'Brien draws back a little from the bars.

"You must see to my immediate release, Brother," says Donough. His tone carries in it that undeniable mixture that is request superseded by command. He looks deep and long into the whiteness of Benignus' eyes, but can, of course, see nothing in them that speaks either of obedience or defiance.

"I think not, my lord." Donough knows that Benignus speaks out of concern for his well-being, but he is, nonetheless, more than a little taken aback by the directness of the monk's response. "It is by far a better thing, Prince Donough," continues the blind one, "that you remain within the safety of these walls."

"But I am their true leader, Brother," retorts the nobleman. "This battle is of the Clan O'Brien, not of some evil-driven lieutenant who has lost the run of himself."

"My Lord Donough, you must listen to me and listen hard and carefully." There is a strange authority and sense of the foreboding in this caution from the monk. "True, Feardorcha is not of the O'Brien, but neither is he of any human kind. His loyalty is not to an earthly master and his only interest, on this or any other day, is to destroy, not to serve. And there is nothing you can do to alter the course of what is now to come."

Donough bows his head. Deep within himself he knows the wisdom in all that Benignus says, just as he also realises the righteousness of this gentle monk who had earlier cautioned him against doing battle in the first place. But, equally, Donough knows that that is of the past and has been overtaken at this point by even more serious happenings.

"You must stay here, my lord, within the sanctuary of the monastery," Benignus tells him. "And when all is done, you will be but one of very few remaining within whose breast there still beats a heart."

And with that, the holy man is gone from the oaken door. Gone to do what he knows must be done. Gone to do that which only he can do.

* * *

Out on the field, where the opposing forces will engage, the mist has lifted appreciably and, at a slight remove, Prince Dermot and his officers have been in discussion. They have left the main body of the men and retreated to an earthen fort that lends itself well to the privacy that is needed for such talk, but which, at the same time, allows for look-outs to stand on its circular elevated bank and watch for the beginnings of matters on the open battlefield. Though none of their number has any intimate knowledge of where it is they stand, there is a palpable sense about them that this place whispers echoes of generations past, that it breathes the names and seed of men who, like themselves, may have left this dwelling place to go into battle, perhaps never to return.

Dermot stands within the circle which his seated men have formed around him. His eyes move smoothly from officer to officer, scanning, heartening, steeling them for the carnage that he knows to lie ahead.

"Men of Thomond," he says, then pauses, and his words, at first, might all too readily be mistaken as nothing but a form of address to his lieutenants. But then he adds to them. "Men of Thomond," he repeats, "is what we are." And he breathes deeply, his chest swelling with its intake of the Burren air and with a sense of pride in those who sit attentively around him. "And as men of Thomond," he continues, "we are brave and we are loyal and we are of the Gael. We are the sons of the sons of sons who have been noble for more generations back than any here can ever think to number." And again he pauses in his speech and smoothly works his listeners with his eyes. "Our fathers and our fathers' fathers were of O'Briens and Mahons, of Considines and Ó Dálaighs and of others of the proudest names of Thomond. And many's the time in years gone by they sat on days like this and prayed their good Lord Saviour Jesus Christ would look down on them as they marched forth into battle. That He would spare them from the death to which the many who would fight around them would most surely be doomed. And if they themselves were not to be spared, they prayed harder that the ends that they might meet would be swift and clean and, above all else, painless."

His words grow on themselves and are swept on passion's wings. They spill from his mouth with an ease that seems to make them independent of any thinking that may play within his mind. Like those to whom he speaks, he too is of Thomond and the Gael, but maybe even more so than any of his listeners. And his gift of fiery speech is what has come down to him from those who have trodden the paths of battle for years before him. And, indeed, it is this very gift that will pass from him in time and issue from the mouths of others in generations not yet even thought of.

And seated in the gathering is young Iarla and, alongside him, the ever-solid Riordan. Their eyes are turned up in their heads as they watch the valiant Dermot wheel about the circle, his commanding style and energy engaging each and every man around him, instilling in them that very pride and passion which he himself exudes. Iarla is mindful that, on several previous occasions throughout his childhood, he has heard Dermot deliver in this way. But this, he is all too well aware, is the first time that both father and son will have gone onto the field of battle together in a common cause. For not the only time in a brace of hours, Iarla's thoughts turn to the possibility that this may yet be a day of days, that one or other of them may not see the light of dawn again when all is done. And then, indeed, creeps in the even darker thought that neither man may do so.

"Beirigí dóchas agus beirigí bua, a fheara," urges Dermot, as he attempts with his choice of words to instill in his men's consciousness the belief that victory will follow if they are positive of heart and mind. *"An lámh láidir in uachtar,"* the chieftain adds, issuing the motto so cherished by the Clan O'Brien.

"Dóchas agus bua, dóchas agus bua," the troops chant, reiterating the essence of Dermot's message that hope and victory are intrinsically entwined. And the cacophony of their voices carries out beyond the earthen bank of the fort, reaching the ears and hearts of their troops where they await their officers' return.

"Dóchas agus bua, dóchas agus bua," the call comes back – and again, and again. Dermot and his men within the fort think, at first, that this is simply the echo of their own shouting, but, in little time at all, they realise that it is something more, something greater, something they have not expected. All are quickly on their feet and they move from the middle of the fort up on to its elevated rampart. And what they see before them would, they know, fill even the dullest of hearts at the very worst of times. Dermot's troops beyond out on the battlefield have, to the very last man, risen to their feet and are pumping their weapons in the air, as they chant the inspiring words first issued from their leader's lips. And the officers along the bank look at one another and are filled in their belief that no man from amongst their ranks will be found wanting on this day.

But Dermot's keenness of intellect impresses on him that – like Iarla's earlier observation regarding Feardorcha's working of his troops' minds – such enthusiasm must be quelled before it reaches fever pitch. He knows that if it is not curbed at this point it will be impossible to sustain it until the time of battle. He holds his arms up high in an attempt to calm the men, but such is their distance from him that they interpret his action as a gesture of approval of their chanting and, rather than having the desired effect, they are driven nearer to euphoria. Realising what is happening now, Dermot is just about to instruct his officers to quickly get amongst the men when one of the look-outs who has been posted on the bank since the outset of the meeting intervenes.

"Prince Dermot, Prince Dermot," he shouts, and the sense of alarm in his calling gains the leader's immediate attention.

"The Abbey field," shouts the look-out, and he points beyond the place where the chieftain's troops are gathered. Dermot screws his eyes and looks hard into the distance, and then those very eyes widen at what it is they see. The forces of Prince Donough march forth in battle sections, some already spilling over dividing walls and moving with purpose to the flanks on either side. And Dermot and all around him can clearly see that, to the fore, it is Feardorcha who leads them.

"What of Donough?" asks Iarla, turning first to his father and then to Riordan.

Riordan's and Prince Dermot's eyes momentarily lock hard on one another and then they break their stare.

"That is for another day, Master Iarla," says Riordan. "Now, let us move in haste."

"To the men," barks Dermot, and his officers immediately respond to his instruction. They move at speed out across the field ahead, each hurriedly heading for the division for which he is responsible.

"Iarla," shouts Dermot, as he sees his son head off with the other officers. The young man stops and looks back at his father who still stands on the bank of the fort. Then they move towards each other and embrace. They hold each other tightly, the younger realising that the law of averages may work against his father and the older knowing even more that war is no respecter of life, be one young or old. Then Dermot eases Iarla away from him.

"Take this, my son," he says, as he reaches his hand in under his breastplate, removes a leather pouch and hands it to the younger man.

Iarla looks at the pouch, then at his father, then at the pouch again.

"It came to me from your forebearer, Turlough, whom you never knew, and now it is for you to carry it a while. And when it comes time that you should pass it to your own son, I pray you'll have the wisdom and opportunity to do so."

Iarla makes to remove the contents from the pouch, but his father interrupts him.

"No," says Dermot, closing his hand firmly down on that of his son. "It is not for now," he tells him. "Place it beneath your breastplate and carry it with you as I have done for all these years past." And he looks lovingly but hard into Iarla's blue eyes. His mother's eyes. "Now go," says Dermot, steeling himself against the feelings that are playing with his heart. "There is warring to be done."

With that, the father eases the hold that is grip on grip, then presses the freed hand hard against his son's back and sends him on his way. And, looking after the young man as he goes, Dermot now raises hand to eye, but not in time to stop the falling tear …

14

All hopes that the sun, in time, might manage to totally defeat the mist have come to nought. Indeed, now, as the opposing forces draw up and manoeuvre themselves into their battle positions, the gloom seems once again to have fallen as heavily as at any point before. Leaders of divisions in the respective armies are at the head of their men and all await the coming together in the middle of the battlefield of the two opposing cousins, Dermot and Donough, the princes of the divided Clan O'Brien.

For Dermot's officers, their arrival at the front of their divisions has been somewhat more rushed than they might have liked, their hurrying from the fort having been prompted by the unexpected entrance of the enemy forces onto the battlefield. Not only is their composure less than what they might have it be, but any previous thoughts that archers on the flanks or troops of swoop and plunder might be used by Iarla as a surprise element have already been banished by the suddenness of action of Prince Donough's forces.

Iarla watches as his father rides out gently from the ranks to meet his cousin Donough in the centre of the field. He is surprised, as is Dermot himself, to see, however, that it is the spear-bearing Feardorcha – not Donough – who approaches from the opposite side, the weighted rolled hem of the silvery coat of mail that drapes his black stallion brushing the dewy wetness of the grass as he moves. Why Feardorcha, wonder father and son.

"Why Feardorcha?" whispers Riordan to himself, as he too looks on. And as the words issue from the stalwart's lips, the riders are seen to stop, one before the other, their horses' noses all but touching, the whitened shafts of breath from the animals' flaring nostrils pumping out against the dampness of the gloom.

"My cousin does not even do me the honour of facing me before going into battle, then," says Dermot. The tone of his remark is very obviously much more in the nature of rebuke than it is observation.

"Your cousin, my lord, and what honour he does or does not do you is no longer of any consequence on this day."

Dermot smarts at the impertinence of Feardorcha's response. He is little more than half of Dermot's age and, despite his high rank in Prince Donough's army, little is, or ever has been, known of him other than the fact that he most certainly is not of any Gaelic clan. "It is I who give you battle here, sir," continues the lieutenant, "not some wilting old man who would sooner see you mend your differences in the cause of restoring harmony within your family."

"But I have no –"

"Enough," barks Feardorcha, cutting into Dermot's speech. "I have had enough of the talk and reasoning of the O'Briens, whatever be their side. My only business here is in the cause of making war." Then each man's stare meets the other's. And that fastening of eyes is of a faltering and yielding blue on ever-hardening black.

"And so, to the fight," snaps Feardorcha, and he drives his spear down hard into the ground beside where Dermot's horse is standing. Then he jerks his stallion's reins, turns and races back towards his cheering ranks.

Dermot sits and watches as his adversary gallops off in the direction of his men. Were he not of an age when little can surprise him he might well be shocked that, not only is the army against which his men will do battle several times the size of his own, but it is also headed by a leader other than his cousin. At one and the same time he takes the strain on the reins, drawing his horse's head a little to one side, gently turns his heels into its flanks and makes back to join his troops. And as he moves away, the clamour from Feardorcha's army rolls and threatens, builds and rumbles on itself until the noise is deafening.

Seeing the ardour and enthusiasm of the enemy before them, Dermot's own forces intuitively realise the necessity to respond in kind and they too now begin to roar their cries of battle. Within seconds Dermot sees that his men are already moving towards him and, when he looks around to view the opposition, he realises that their adversaries are coming down the field at speed. This time he digs his heels hard into his horse's flanks and makes more hastily towards his oncoming men. He thinks to raise his arm and halt his troops' approach, but his soldier's mind quickly tells him that this would spell nothing but disaster for them. It would, he knows, throw all things into confusion and could not possibly bode well for his side's chances were he to do so.

As Dermot nears his now onrushing men, he checks his steed a little, reducing him from gallop to mere canter. Then a second check of the reins and the animal is little more than walking. And then, so as to ensure that he will be at the head of affairs in engaging Feardorcha's dark forces, Dermot makes to turn his horse to face them. But as the chieftain of this one half of the Clan O'Brien does so, a spear, already hurtling towards him, foully meets its target and embeds itself into the flesh of Dermot's side. It enters hard and deep at that very point where the breast and backplates of his armour ever fail to meet, easily piercing the light mail tunic immediately beneath the fashioned sheets of metal and causing the vest's tiny iron rings to instantly drip red. He is jolted, stunned, but then, most strangely, a creeping calmness takes command of him. And for some seconds, the chieftain's awareness of the world is much keener than at any time in life that he can remember.

But then a change. It is a change that is as sudden in its nature as was the jolt that he had felt. Now he is oblivious to the clamour that engulfs him. He looks to either side and his vision – no longer keen – suggests to him that both bands of soldiers are moving serenely towards him. They seem to come in a motion that is slow, and they are joyous to his eye, laughing, revelling in the prospect of encounter, as would a brother who comes openly to meet with brother. But, as suddenly as came the change, the injury bites even harder than before and what has been a temporary imagining reverts now to an even greater sense of pain than he had felt when first the spear had entered his side.

Yet another change in consciousness. The clamour now is roaring in Dermot's head and he is more aware than ever of what it is that's happening around him. A third bite within and he feels a tightening of his innards and a rolling pain moves upwards towards his chest. The pain seems at first to envelop his heart and lungs, almost as though hands of comfort have come to ease his trouble. But very

their headlong rush towards the enemy. They move at
speed and, to the fore, held aloft for friend and foe to see,
is the banner bearing the insignia of this ancient clan of
Thomond. These are men committed to the last. Men
committed to the cause of the O'Brien.

The frontlines of the armies will make their first
encounter in that saucer of land that is sometimes lake and
sometimes not, where downslope meets with downslope,
entrapping all things into a hollow. Iarla, still in the clutches
of Riordan, shifts his gaze back to that point on the field
where he had seen his father slump forward on his mount.
The horse stands alone as some of the O'Brien soldiers,
who had left the ranks to tend to their now dead leader, are
seen to carry Dermot's body back towards the seclusion of
the earthen fort – the very fort where earlier his gift of
speech had so inspired his men. Iarla averts his gaze and
looks deeply into Riordan's green eyes. And then he moves
his right hand in beneath the breastplate of his armour and
feels the rock-hard object within the pouch which earlier
his father had given to him.

"The O'Brien," the young chieftain says, this time with
a fervour and resolve that was not there till now. And as he
speaks the words, he digs the fingertips of his left hand
deep into his lieutenant's upper arm. Then, releasing his
hold on Riordan, he eyes the distant horse again and makes
off in its direction.

As Iarla reaches his father's horse, he looks over to the
scene of battle. Already the armies have engaged each
other and troops fight toe to toe in the centre of the hollow.
He sees Riordan to the fore in the encounter now, flailing
and scything all that comes into his path. A moving gauze

of vapour rises from the warrior and from the bodies of those who fight and lie dead and wounded all around him. Childhood images from stories told him by his father of the mighty Cú Chulainn of the North momentarily flash across Iarla's mind. Then he shifts his gaze beyond the centre of the fray and sees, in the distance, on slightly higher land, near to the stone pen where earlier that morning he and his men had holed up a while, the solitary and foreboding figure of the black-clad Feardorcha. The dark lieutenant is seated on his stallion, overlooking all that's happening below.

Iarla thinks a moment that the best that he might do would be to make directly for the pen and engage Feardorcha in combat, hand to hand, one to one. But as quickly as comes that thought to mind, there visits with it the memory of those times when, as a boy, his father would remind him that, at crucial moments in his battles to defend the noble province of Uladh, even the great Cú Chulainn had had need of help.

Iarla breaks his focus on the leader of the enemy and his eyes again locate the figure of brave Riordan. He is a giant amongst the others and his wild red hair and beard make it easy for the onlooker's eye to pick him out. The soldier flails and scythes just like before. And to all sides of him, as many again as had previously been the case have yielded to the sword, their life's blood reddening the grass where they have fallen. But already Iarla can tell that many more of his men have met their fate than have their foes. And yet again his father's words in their ancient Gaelic tongue course through his mind: '*Fiú Cú Chulainn féin, thuig sé gan eiteach a thabhairt don chúnamh*' – that foreboding caution that even Cú Chulainn himself could not deny the need of help.

With a speed bewildering to the eye, Iarla grabs the pommel of the saddle with his left hand and athletically hauls himself onto his dead father's horse. Tightening his grip on the reins, he momentarily pulls the animal's head back towards him, draws his sword out of its scabbard, then sits bold and upright on the steed. His awareness of the man whose place he now occupies could not be greater than it is at this very moment. His chest fills with a pride in all that has been, all that is, all that will be in time yet to come.

"The O'Brien!" he bellows, summoning every measure of breath from within his swollen lungs. Then man and horse surge forward to the fray.

As Iarla nears the heat of battle, he sees young Caltra hard-pressed in an effort to fend off two of the aggressors. The youth who, in the space of some small few hours, has been cruelly forced to grow from boy to man, is fighting valiantly but vainly. Iarla checks his horse in gallop, causing it to jar abruptly as it stops. The animal rears up on its hindlegs, neighing sharply as it does so, then the steed is immediately steered off by its rider in the direction of the troubled youngster.

Shifting his sword in mid-gallop from right hand to his left, Iarla draws back his fighting arm as he approaches Caltra's assailants. Then, with a venom given impetus by the speed at which his steed is moving, the chieftain sweeps his arm in a perfect arc and, on the upward swing, his weapon's blade makes deadly contact with the first of the attackers, cutting the unsuspecting soldier right through. The pace at which both horse and man have moved has carried them well beyond Caltra's second adversary.

But now Iarla turns the animal, eyes the youngster's remaining attacker and points his sword directly at his target. The horse rears up on its hindlegs as it had done earlier and, once its front hooves hit the ground again, it surges forward. Iarla's fully outstretched arm and sword are one, and when the weapon's point makes contact with the soldier's chest, a shrill and solitary cry issues out into the Burren air, and the kill is as swift as it is clean and merciless.

The chieftain slides his sword back into its scabbard, then extends his fighting arm towards his comrade. "Come, Caltra," he says, and no sooner said than the young man grabs his leader's arm and is hauled up behind him on the horse's back. Then they make off with fervour towards the very eye of battle.

As the mounted duo head for the spot where Riordan still stands, wielding his mighty sword in sweeping circular fashion and felling all and any who dare to come within its compass, it becomes glaringly obvious to them that few others of their men are holding their ground as successfully as he. With the exception of those put to the sword by the sterling red-haired lieutenant, by far the greater number of those already slain are from Iarla's ranks. In their approach, both Caltra and Iarla jab and swipe, adding to the numbers of the enemy fallen.

By the time they reach Riordan and dismount to stand and fight alongside him, it is all too apparent to them that they, by now, are of the comparatively few of their own

men who are still standing. Iarla glances left and right,
and when opportunity allows, looks quickly to the rear,
feverishly trying to take account of what their numbers are.
Two hundred, he thinks, two hundred and fifty at most.
And in front of them, hordes of Feardorcha's infantrymen
still number in their thousands. And, more ominous again,
behind the infantry are cavalry who range across the field
and on the higher ground, where the fertile earth is eaten
up by rock, stand rows of archers, none of whom have as
yet been pressed into service.

"Your thinking, Riordan?" asks Iarla quickly, as both
men brace themselves for the onset of respective foes. An
immediate lunge forward with his sword and Riordan runs
his opponent through, puts his foot down hard on the
fallen soldier's chest and extricates the blade from the dead
man's belly. Then, as if unthinkingly, he jabs the freed-up
weapon at the infantryman who has engaged Iarla and fells
him on the spot.

"Things are less than good, Master Iarla, and likely to
get worse." The statement is bald and one of fact. There is
neither anxiety nor despair in Riordan's answer. This, for
him, is part of what being a soldier is about. One wins, one
loses, one cuts and one gets cut and, someday, given the
nature of the business that he is about, one will die, and
this is something that he knows. "Retreat to the earthen fort
may become our only option," he adds, as he sees another
of the enemy make for him.

"They come like bees in swarm," says Iarla, as he too
engages a fresh opponent. Again each man quickly makes
the kill and Riordan looks to the far side of Iarla where
young Caltra is fighting like a lion.

"Look beyond, Master," says Riordan, nodding in the boy's direction, and the chieftain does as he is bade.

"Aye, Caltra!" Iarla says. "Boy to man to warrior with little time for thought to any."

Then, most curiously, an order is barked out from a distance and the forces of Feardorcha cease to fight and immediately back away into the ranks of the cavalry. Iarla and Riordan lower their weapons and, bewildered, look towards each other. Then they shift their gaze to the pen beside which, all this time, Feardorcha has remained seated on his horse, overseeing all. Was it he who issued the command, they wonder. But there is little time to spend on wonder, as Iarla and those of his men who have survived the cut gather together and look on in confusion from the centre of the hollow. They are no more than one hundred now, and maybe fewer.

"Look, Master Iarla," says Caltra, his eyes widening as he points towards the enemy ranks.

And, as chieftain and Riordan and each and every man of those still standing turn their gaze towards Feardorcha's army, the lines of cavalry are seen to split rank and from behind them a team of four work-horses emerges, drawing the now uncovered mighty cauldron of oil. The flames still dance upon the metal plate beneath the great pot's belly, but now the fire leaps even more vigorously than before and the oil within the vessel bubbles violently and with viscous venom.

Iarla and Riordan again look at each other. "What is this, Riordan?" the chieftain asks.

"I do not know," says the lieutenant, looking back to the cauldron and screwing up his eyes in an effort to make sense of something which he has never before encountered on the field of battle.

Once in front of the lines of cavalry, the team of horses draws to a halt and a lone member of the division dismounts and leaves his comrades. He reaches the team of four and gathers in the reins. Then, holding the lengthy leather straps in one hand, he climbs the wooden retaining frame which prevents the cauldron from toppling, and sits high up on a crossbeam. Once there, the horseman looks back towards the stone pen and, seeing this, both Iarla and Riordan do likewise. And there, before the gaze of all, is Feardorcha, seated on his stallion. The dark lieutenant raises his left arm, holds it aloft for several seconds, then brings it down suddenly and sharply by his side. And, immediately, the man atop of the wooden frame lashes down hard with the reins, twice in quick succession, the leather scorching first the hindquarters of the front pair and then those to the rear.

There is a collective whinny as the cavalryman leaps from the structure and the team of horses moves forward, jolting the wooden frame and causing a little of the boiling oil to spill out over the rim of the massive cauldron. And as it spills, a gauze of whitened vapour rises from the pot where the liquid within its bowels has been disturbed.

"A vapour," exclaims the onlooking Iarla.

"Vapour, my lord," says Riordan, "and, worse than that, the very liquid which causes such vapour to rise up out of that cauldron."

Iarla looks inquiringly at his officer.

"Boiling oil, Master Iarla, as used by the Persians against their enemies before the very time of Christ."

The words have little time to register in Iarla's mind as both cauldron and team of four trundle down into the hollow. He and his men are scurrying to either side, out of the path of the hurtling vessel, when Iarla again looks towards the distant Feardorcha. Yet again, the enemy leader's arm is raised and he himself is looking towards the row of archers on the higher ground, off onto his right. And so shifts the gaze of Iarla.

Imminence and possibility meet each other in the chieftain's mind and, just as he watches the bowmen raise their weapons of bent hazel towards the sky, Iarla sees the flaming heads of the arrows that they are straining to release. A quick glance at the cauldron once again and, as he looks, Iarla sees that as the team of horses reaches the lowest point within the hollow and makes for the upward gradient, the wooden frame behind them will make contact with the ground. And then Feardorcha drops his arm down to his side – and possibility and imminence inevitably conspire to make reality.

Even before the fire-burning arrows reach their target, the cauldron has spewed the contents of its belly out into the hollow. The flames that hitherto have danced on the iron underplate spread themselves effusively, meeting the inward weaving blaze created to the sides where the hail of arrows still incessantly showers down. Iarla and his men are trapped, oil washing warm around their ankles and getting warmer, flames galloping from all sides, and some already screaming out in pain at the horror that engulfs them. The water-table of underlying limestone ensures that most of the viscous liquid stays above the surface and escape from this seems of the realm of fantasy.

Quick of mind, and even quicker still of limb, Riordan grabs the broken reins of one of the team of four as the frantic animal attempts to hasten past him. The jolt he feels almost tears his arm out of its socket, but he holds fast, holds firm, stubborn to the last. The horse is halted in its gallop and Riordan throws himself onto its back, gathers the split reins and turns both self and animal to look for Iarla. Flame now is their most threatening enemy. Bodies writhe and squirm in frenzy-driven pain in the pond of burning oil. It is as though some phosphoric leech has attached itself to them and is gnawing relentlessly through their flesh and into their very bones. The ever-loyal lieutenant picks out his chieftain from amongst the many who are writhing in agony as fire claims them for its own. Both Iarla and Caltra stand together, trying in vain to rescue those for whom hope is dwindling fast.

Riordan eyes his master and then Caltra, momentarily draws back the horse's head and surges forward through the inferno. "Iarla," he roars, as he nears the chieftain, his left arm extended so as to enable him to grab hold of his master and pull him up behind him on the horse's back. But Iarla cannot conceive of abandoning his men like this. His look is one of confusion and he does not reach out his arm to take hold of the onrushing Riordan's. And Riordan passes him with speed and then turns back.

"Caltra, boy," he says, now offering his arm to the youth.

The youngster, though having shown qualities of courage remarkable in one of such tender years, is less able to resist the offer. He eyes the mounted Riordan, feels the flames around his feet and is increasingly aware of the

intensity of heat as they creep up the leather gaiters that
protect his shins. He knows that staying where he is means
to be eaten by the fire and that then he will be of little use
to anyone. Instinctively, he takes the lieutenant's arm and
is hauled onto the animal's back.

"Iarla," barks Riordan once again. Iarla turns, his two
hands clutching the tunic of a soldier who has already
yielded to the flames. And the two men's eyes meet. "It is
folly, Master," shouts the officer. "Think of all that is yet to
be done. Think of your father. Of your kingdom. What
sense that you should be eaten by the fire? Feardorcha's
fire." The words come from Riordan's lips as lashingly as
come the arrows that still fuel the leaping flames. Iarla
tightens his mouth, hardens his stare at his lieutenant.
"Think of the Lady Sorcha," says Riordan then. And this
last of his attempts is that which finally hits home with the
young chieftain. He does not even think to wonder at how
Riordan might ever have known anything of him and
Sorcha. He eases his hold on the soldier's tunic and the
dead man falls away from him. "Now, Iarla," says Riordan,
and both he and Caltra thrust their arms out towards their
young leader. Iarla feels the heat creep up his legs with far
greater intensity than he had felt when he had been
preoccupied with the saving of his men. Decisively, he
reaches out his arm, grabs that of Caltra, then he too is
pulled onto the horse's back. And, immediately, animal
and men rush off through the burning oil and make for the
higher ground.

It is only the speedy and continuous movement of the
horse's legs that saves its fetlocks from being scorched by
any single flame. In a matter of seconds, it has taken the

trio out beyond the hollow and on to the higher ground. Once there, Riordan turns the horse so that they may view the carnage from which they have fled. The scene is harrowing for them to behold. Iarla is the first to slip down off the hindquarters of the animal, then Caltra, while Riordan stays mounted on the horse, leans forward on its neck and sighs a sigh that speaks its own account.

All is silent. The O'Brien chieftain crouches low, propping himself by pressing his closed fist hard against the earth beneath. His eyes pan the ugliness of the oil-filled depression, now some distance from him. No noise, even from Feardorcha's forces who still look on at a distance from the hollow. And nothing stirs. Nothing but the smoke that rises from the charred and viscous-seeping mounds of fallen human flesh. And the smell. The smell is that of burning meat – one more commonly associated in the chieftain's mind with times of merriment, when food and mead and company would make for celebration.

No celebration here. No gaiety. No life. And the company that is Iarla's is so whittled down in number that fewer than the fingers that go to make two hands are needed to take full measure of it. They are but three, and then the other four who earlier had carried the body of the fallen Dermot back to the seclusion of the earthen fort. Iarla draws breath into his lungs, the inhalation soured by the acrid smell of burning that is on the air. In some strange way, the intake seems to serve to stifle his mounting tears. He looks back at Riordan. There is a vacancy in the old war dog's eyes. He seems so stilled by all of this that, if he has nodded at his chieftain, the act has been so lifeless that it has gone unseen. Iarla then shifts his gaze and, this time,

15

Some hours have passed. It is not the gloomy grey of cloud that marks the day now but the approaching dark of night. Within the fort, none is more surprised than Iarla and Riordan that Feardorcha has afforded them the time and reverence to bury Dermot inside the embanked enclosure. Though drawn up in ranks outside and ready for attack, the dark one and his troops have, all this time, stayed a respectful distance from the fort. It has been strange that, a little earlier, as the kneeling Iarla rose to his feet by the wet and clingy mound of clay under which his father has been placed, a white dove flew into the ancient dwelling place. It had perched itself on one side of the crossbeam of the crude wooden crucifix that the young O'Brien had fashioned for the dead one's grave. And, having rested there a while, the bird of peace flew up into the branches of one of the many trees that pepper the earthen rampart of the fort.

"You have done well by your father, Iarla," says Riordan, closing his bucket of a hand on the young man's wrist as they sit by the campfire which they have built in the middle of the settlement. Caltra and three of the other four sit around the burning logs and fear and flame consort with each other and dance lively in their eyes.

"No more, Riordan, my loyal friend, than I would want a son should do for me."

"Aye!" says Riordan, and he breathes out hard against the dampness of the night air.

"Master Iarla, Master Iarla," comes a shout of obvious

anxiety from the embankment. It is the voice of Cuanán, the fourth of the men who had carried Dermot's body back to the fort. He has been there as look-out since replacing another of the four some time earlier. All six around the campfire rise and make hastily towards him.

"What is it, Cuanán?" asks Riordan, reaching him before any of the others.

"See," the look-out says, pointing out into the darkness and tracing three or four paths of burning torchlight that seem to move in haste in different directions.

"They are coming," says Iarla, who by now has drawn up by Riordan's side. "Caltra, to the west end of the fort," instructs The O'Brien. "You men, at the entrance to the settlement," he tells the other three, and immediately all move as directed.

"Good work, Cuanán," says Riordan, and he and Iarla crouch low against the bank of earth to see if they can discern a pattern to the enemy's approach. And as they do so, a solid processsion of moving torchlight is seen to start marching directly towards them.

"Some move in split ranks right and left, as marauders, Iarla," says Riordan, "but the main force is coming at us down the middle."

"Aye," says Iarla, raising a finger to his lips in signal to Riordan to say nothing else for now. "Stand firm as you are, Cuanán," the chieftain says, and he draws Riordan with him back into the centre of the fort. They stand at opposite sides of the blazing fire, each holding his hands over the flames and feeling the pain of a snide and creeping dampness being driven from their bones. Despite the dancing merriment of light weaving uncertain patterns on them, their faces seem heavy with concern.

"We are few, very few, Riordan, my friend, and Feardorcha's men are in their thousands."

"Yes, Iarla, this is so, but that may be as much to our advantage as it is otherwise."

"I hear what you are saying, Riordan, but I cannot pretend that I fully understand."

"Iarla," says Riordan, lowering himself onto his hunkers and indicating to The O'Brien to do likewise at the other side of the fire. Twice now Iarla has noticed how Riordan has called him only by the name given him at christening. No use of 'lord' or 'master' at this point, and that is how Iarla himself would best have it. He knows it is occasioned by the rapid closeness that has developed between them and, greater still, by a mutual and immeasurable respect. "What must be safeguarded above all else is the seed of the O'Brien."

Iarla looks questioningly at his lieutenant, inviting Riordan to expound on what it is that he is saying.

"Fully one half of the Clan O'Brien will be leaderless and dead should you not come safely from the fray that is to happen here," says Riordan. "You are the seed of a generation yet to come and, as such, the seed of seeds of every future generation of the O'Brien on your side of the name."

Then Riordan, drawing his face as near the leaping flames as one might dare, fixes his chieftain hard with his stare. And Iarla can see in the greenness of the officer's dancing eyes that, ultimately, nothing will be other than the way that Riordan calls it.

"What sense for you to die if such is not necessary?"

asks Riordan. And before Iarla can even ask what it is that his lieutenant is suggesting, the wily warrior continues. "If you can escape from here unknown, then that is the course that you must take. You –"

"But, Riordan, to run away from this and leave my –"

"No, Iarla," interrupts Riordan very firmly. "No, Master," he says then, taking any suggestion of impertinence out of his initial crossing of the young chieftain's speech. "Not to run from, but rather to run to. You run to ensure the future of your people."

"But, Riordan," begins Iarla again. But almost as quickly as he does so, the officer overrides his words for a second time.

"It is your duty, Iarla. It is your duty, just as it is mine to tell you so. Loyalty to things can, at times, blind one to what is right and sensible. Courage, you know, oft times unwittingly leads one to take the lesser option. You, my friend, lack for neither of these noble traits."

Iarla listens attentively to Riordan. No thought now to interrupt him as he did before. There is a wisdom and a pace to what the lieutenant is imparting to him and, though less than half the other's age, Iarla is sufficiently perceptive to realise that this is the case.

"There is little in this world that one can say to be of greater importance than are loyalty and courage," says Riordan, "but that which I have said – the carrying on of the name – is, indeed, such a thing."

Iarla looks into the playing yellow of the fire. In a way, the flames' suggested uncertainty is not unlike the dancing of the thoughts within his mind. He knows that all that Riordan says is born of sense, that it is rational, that it is said with a selflessness that is nothing other than that which he, and indeed his father, would expect of the man. But, nonetheless, it is hard for the young leader to reconcile the notion of leaving the situation, even in the name of greater good.

"There is the entrance to a souterrain within this settlement, Iarla, a passageway that runs beneath the fort and exits somewhere out beyond it," Riordan tells him.

"A souterrain!" says Iarla.

"Yes, my friend. It is within the circle, towards the west end of the place and just some paces from where Caltra is now standing," and, as Riordan tells him this, both men look in the direction of the raw youth who is still stationed on the embankment. "Come," says Riordan, and he makes to rise and bring the young O'Brien to the spot of which he speaks.

"Men closing on two sides," shouts Cuanán from his sentry post. There is decided alarm in the announcement.

Iarla and Riordan abandon thoughts of things discussed for now and make back immediately to where Cuanán is. The look-out is showing signs of nervousness, his eyes flitting hither and thither like those of a frightened animal that have been caught by the light of burning torches in the night. And, despite the sentry's remove from the campfire, the beads of sweat that swamp his face catch the yellow of its distant flames.

"Keep firm, Cuanán," says Iarla, closing his hand tightly on the soldier's upper arm. "Remember that you are of the MacNamara and that there is none as great as are your people at a time of danger." Cuanán looks into Iarla's eyes and is instantly steeled by the resolve he sees in them.

"Men approaching from the west," comes a fresh shout. This time the call is that of Caltra, at the opposite side of the fort. Both Riordan and Iarla look across the enclosure.

"It is best that you should stay with Cuanán, Iarla," says Riordan. "I will go to Caltra." And the lieutenant moves with speed across the centre of the settlement and throws himself against the bank where Caltra has been keeping watch.

"See," says the youngster, pointing out to where a stream of moving torches can be seen to weave a windy course against the rise of land that nears the fort. Riordan tightens his eyes against the challenge of the darkness.

"They are twelve in number, maybe fifteen," says Riordan.

"Aye," Caltra confirms, "and that is only if each man is the bearer of a torch."

Riordan does not respond, but he knows well that Caltra's observation may be all too true. Were the situation not so pressing, the seasoned soldier might well take the time to think how remarkably quickly Caltra is learning the trade of soldiering. At least fifteen, Riordan knows, and more than likely twice as many. But he shares nothing of those thoughts with the youth.

"Hold true, young Caltra," Riordan says, "and I will be back with you within the minute." Then Riordan races hard across the enclosure once again and reaches Iarla.

"Men closing from the west, Iarla. A score and ten in number, at the very least."

"How many here then, Riordan?" asks the chieftain, nodding towards the numbers approaching on the eastern side. Again Riordan tightens his eyes and takes account of the burning torches. He sighs.

"As many again," he says, "and most probably more than that."

"And what of the entrance to the fort?" asks Iarla, his mind now racing feverishly in an effort to think of all that must be considered. Instinctively, both men press themselves back up off the embankment and look towards the entrance where the other three of their number have been stationed.

"Cuanán, we leave a while, but only for some minutes," Iarla assures the sentry. "Keep low behind the bank and, if there is need to shout, do not delay in doing so." Cuanán nods, tucks himself into a little niche in the inner side of the rampart and, as Riordan and his chieftain leave him, he strains his eyes to watch the movement outside.

When they reach the entrance, there is no sign of any of the three. Iarla is amazed that they should have abandoned their posts in this fashion. Both men search, as best as light allows, to the right and left, and even venture outside the fort a little to look for traces of the soldiers.

"Nothing, Riordan," says Iarla, the tone of dejection in his voice saying all that he is thinking.

"It is not what you may suspect, Iarla. These are not men who even think to know the colour of cowardice. They are soldiers of the fight, whose loyalty and courage run even deeper than the very marrow of their bones. The name of the O'Brien, your father's memory and now you yourself command that loyalty in them. This is something other than that which seems to be the case. This –"

And suddenly, Riordan's speech is interrupted by the cooing of the dove high up in the branches, where earlier it had sought to perch itself. Both men raise their eyes and, as they do so, their attention is immediately caught by a sight most ominous in nature. Overhead, hanging from the boughs of the two great oaks that form an archway over the entrance to the fort, are the missing three. Their bodies sway to and fro a little and, as Iarla and Riordan stand in under them and look directly upwards, each is momentarily blinded by the thick red droplets that fall down into their eyes. They step back, wipe their men's lifeblood from their faces and lift their eyes again. What uncertain light there is suffices for them to realise that the hanging of these men has been the least of the discomfort that has been dealt them in their meeting with their doom. Dangling from the bodies are torn and dripping strips of flesh that have been the doing of something that is surely less than human.

Both chieftain and lieutenant draw their short-blade knives and move away from each other to the opposing tree trunks. They have only begun to scale the trees, with the intention of severing the ropes from which the bodies hang, when they hear a cry announce itself out into the night. It comes from the east side of the fort. And, yet again, their course is altered. They slither down the tree trunks and make in haste across the settlement to where Cuanán has been stationed. And there before them, impaled on three thick hazel-handled spears, is the limp and lifeless corpse of the MacNamara son. Cuanán Mac Róigh MacNamara, dead.

Iarla and Riordan lower their heads beneath the upper line of the earthen bank and turn to face each other.

"Caltra!" they both say at the one time. Then Riordan swings his body round to face the western end of the fort.

"Caltra," he shouts, " get inside the fort, boy. Now." The words are hardly out of Riordan's mouth when the youth is seen to leap down off the bank and come running towards them. "Iarla, you must go, my friend," says Riordan, now grabbing his chieftain by the arm.

"No, Riordan, I stay. Or if I go, then you and Caltra must come with me."

Caltra looks on. He knows nothing of the souterrain or of the two men's earlier discussion. In many ways, in his own mind, his rapid growth has been cushioned by the kindness of these two towards him and by the knowledge that they bring to every situation an experience that he has not yet gained.

It has never entered Riordan's thoughts that he too might escape through the souterrain. His soldier's mind has only ever dictated to him that he should always stand his ground and fight. And even now, despite the seed being sown by Iarla's suggestion, Riordan's every instinct tells him that he should reject the notion. His duty is to the safety of The O'Brien and such is his thinking that any personal concern must be subjugated with regard for that.

"If I should go, Riordan, my friend," says Iarla, "what sense be there that you should stay and –"

"Master Iarla," says Caltra, cutting in on his chieftain's words. His face is ashen and drawn, his eyes so wide that it is wonder that their sockets can contain them.

Iarla and Riordan turn. Feardorcha's men swarm across the west bank like a blanket of locusts, black and vast and threatening, and sweep into the centre of the settlement. The three make to brace themselves for what surely must be their final deed, when all is interrupted.

"Halt," rasps a voice that is other than the three and other than any of the soldiers moving towards them. The troops within do as they have been bade, but already more are seen to crawl across the embankment from all sides. They come like snakes, weaving towards the middle of the settlement and carrying the torches that earlier had foretold of their approach. Their number now is huge, nearer to one thousand than to some lesser figure.

Iarla and his companions look to the entrance to the fort, whence the command has come, and there, big and bold between the mighty oaks stands Feardorcha, the dark one. Helmeted, he looks out through the tiny slit in his visor. He holds a sword diagonally across his chest, its hilt clutched tightly in his right hand, the blade held loosely in the mail-clad left.

"You," the dark lieutenant says, pointing the weapon directly at Iarla. "I have come for you." And he eyes the young chieftain hard, despite the distance of two-score paces that there is between them. "I have seen your wretched father to his Maker and now it has come time to do so with you."

Iarla stands out from the bank of earth and, eyes fixed firmly on Feardorcha, he reaches his hand down towards the handle of his sword. And just as the chieftain is about to extract the weapon from its scabbard, Caltra surges past him. The youngster brushes against his leader as he goes by and, with his sword thrust out directly in front of him, he rushes headlong towards Feardorcha.

"The O'Brien," screams the boy, his movement gaining pace as he nears the evil one. But to Feardorcha, this is as would be ice unto a flame. He lets the callow youth come towards him and, with a skill so clearly born of the many times he has engaged such challenge in the past, he extends his fighting arm and sword straight out from him and, at the crucial moment, he steps to one side and allows Iarla's young servant run straight onto the blade.

The youth knows little of what has happened. One single cry of pain and his blood runs as freely as has that of many an honourable warrior this day. Feardorcha lets the youngster fall back onto the ground, the sword buried deep beneath his ribcage. Then he stands over the boy, places his right foot down hard on his chest, clutches the hilt of the weapon with both hands and yanks the bloodied blade out of the body. He holds the blade aloft and lets young Caltra's blood run down the shaft. As the gory stream nears the sword's hilt, Feardorcha lowers the mouth guard of his helmet, tilts his weapon, then places his mouth against its metal and allows the droplets fall onto his tongue. And he emits another of his noises that is not fully human. Then he turns his eyes on Iarla once again.

"You," he says, pointing his sword at the chieftain for a second time. The reflection of the burning torches held high by those who look on in the centre of the settlement dances menacingly in the shiny blackness of Feardorcha's armour. "It is you, The O'Brien, who brings me here and only one of us will leave this place this night. And only one of us will ever again have his way with the daughter of Mahon." And as he deals this latter blow, Feardorcha throws back his head and laughs mockingly at the younger man.

Iarla is incensed, more by this reference to Sorcha than by anything else the dark one has done or said.

Immediately the chieftain unsheathes his sword, but Riordan is quick to act beside him. His lieutenant stands before him, tightly gripping each of his master's wrists and restricting his movement.

"No, Iarla," he tells The O'Brien, "this is nothing but his way of stirring you to foolishness. It is a lie that is built upon a lie and is said only to make you lower your guard. Do not be goaded by him." And Riordan tightens his hold even more, causing Iarla to drop his sword.

"No lie," says Feardorcha. "Neither is it lie upon a lie."

"No," shouts Riordan, turning his head to face the evil one, while still holding Iarla firmly in his grip. Then Riordan throws his master back against the earthen bank, unsheathes his own sword now and lunges forward towards the entrance to the fort. Immediately, several of Feardorcha's men rush towards the chieftain and hold The O'Brien down where he has fallen. Iarla's loyal lieutenant emits a fearsome roar as he makes headlong for his foe and Feardorcha stands at the ready, bracing himself for what he fully knows will be a far greater test of him than was the weakly effort of young Caltra.

The clang of metal against metal rings out around the fort and sparks are seen to hop from one or other of the heavy iron swords. Though Iarla's arms and legs are pinned hard against the bank, he can clearly see the battle that is being fought. Despite their massive frames and mighty strength of limb, the weight of their weapons is such that neither of the men can take two successive swings at his opponent. And summoned from the depths come grunts and groans with every effort. But such is their agility that no man lays his blade upon the other and the only contact made is that of metal upon metal.

For minutes that run rapidly to ten, and then beyond the score, the art of bob-and-weave is seen at its finest and no one of the two can be thought to have gained any form of edge over the other. And all this time, Iarla has been pinned against the ground, his frustration mounting, his wish to aid his comrade growing to frenzy in him. He knows that it will be something other than their skill as swordsmen that will separate the victor from the vanquished in this fray. Something spurious. Something that is less than fair to one or other man. And then it happens.

Riordan has, as every time till now, avoided yet another of Feardorcha's sweeping attempts. The men's arms are tiring with the effort it is taking to sustain the fight and each knows that flagging energy, as much as anything else, might well be his undoing. Riordan lifts his mighty sword, wielding it high above his head. He eyes his target firmly, musters all the strength remaining in his body and unleashes what will be his greatest effort. But Feardorcha, as every time before, sidesteps the threatening weapon and, in his follow-through, Riordan's forged-iron blade bounces off the trunk of one of the majestic portal oaks and breaks in two.

Iarla's lieutenant turns now, half-sword in hand. He realises that the element of mercy cannot be numbered amongst Feardorcha's traits. Indeed, were their roles reversed, Riordan knows full well that he would run the dark one through without a thought. And now Feardorcha nears him, his weapon held high above his left shoulder, ready for the kill. Riordan musters every element of courage that he has within him and he surges forward.

"In the name of the O'Brien," he roars, and, as the final word departs his lips, the blade of Feardorcha's weighty sword sweeps across him, catching him squarely on the neck and beheading him in an instant. And the head sails through the air and well out beyond the confines of the fort, still issuing echoes of the name of the O'Brien onto the wind.

And now that which may prove to be the final act – the deed by which Feardorcha knows all sway held by the Clan O'Brien, whatever be its hue, can be banished for ever more. The dark knight turns to face Iarla.

"Let him up," he barks at those who have kept the chieftain pinned against the earth throughout the slaying of the loyal Riordan. Inside, the young man is torn, distraught at the fate that he has seen meted out to his noble comrade and to young Caltra not long before that again. But he knows, above all else, that he must not allow emotion cloud his vision, that clarity of mind is everything in this situation. Riordan's caution to him that he should not let himself be goaded by anything that Feardorcha may say still courses through his mind. Iarla stands. He knows he must present well, he knows he must be firm, he knows that he cannot be seen to weaken in any way.

"What is it we should call you that you dare to think yourself able for The O'Brien?" The question issues from Iarla's lips with an apparent confidence that gives the lie to the trembling that the young man feels within. Feardorcha himself is a little taken aback by its bluntness and, for a moment, he wonders if perhaps he has underestimated Iarla's mettle.

"Are you so ugly a specimen of man that you cannot

remove your headdress and meet the eye of he who will so reduce you that you will fall down on your knees and beg for mercy?" asks Iarla, intentionally not allowing time for Feardorcha to answer the first question he has thrown at him.

"Or is it to be left to me, when I have run you through, that I should reveal the face that hides behind the metal?" Again the question is issued fast on the heels of the other two and with the sole intention of unsettling his opponent.

Feardorcha is smarting. His anger has been raised, but he is wily in his ways and, much like Iarla, he knows that if he shows he has been irked, he will immediately place himself at a disadvantage in the presence of the other. He lowers his sword, turns away and places it by the oak tree against which Riordan had broken his weapon earlier. Then, turning back to face his adversary, he places his hands on either side of the helmet and lifts it upwards from his head. The bottom rim of the helmet has just cleared Feardorcha's eyes when he is thrown into confusion by the sudden and frenetic flying of a creature around him. The lieutenant has come from darkness into a relative brightness and his eyes have not had time to realise that this is the dove which earlier had sought seclusion in the branches. Feardorcha has made immediately for his sword, tripping over an elevated root as he does so and being made to look somewhat ridiculous. But no sooner has he seized the sword than the bird has flown to the other side of the settlement, leaving those gathered in the middle of the area laughing openly at what has happened. Knowing that he has been made to look foolish in their presence and still irked by the nature of the questions which Iarla has thrown at him, Feardorcha lashes out with venom.

"Out," he barks at his men. "Get out of the fort, one and all of you. Out, out, out."

There is little said amongst the soldiers as they hastily depart the settlement, but, in their hearts, some of their number take secret joy from the fact that Feardorcha has been reduced to the level of a fool. Though they dare not say so, many of these men resent the absence of their leader, Prince Donough, and at this stage would almost more readily give their allegiance to Iarla himself than to the dark pretender. Once outside, they seat themselves to the east of the fort, halfway between its banks and the hollow in which so many of Iarla's men had met their cruel fate earlier in the day. Already they can hear the sound of metal meeting metal back in the enclosure and the beginnings of a wind is felt to mount somewhere to the north of them.

Metal rests hard on metal within the fort itself. Iarla's back is pressed against the earthen rampart, his sword held horizontally across his chest, blocking the blade of Feardorcha's weapon from making contact with him. The two men's faces are within inches of each other and, despite the half-light, The O'Brien can see his opponent's nostrils flare and pulsate in a way not given to any human he has ever seen before. Feardorcha is a much bigger man than he had seemed to be when at a distance, thinks Iarla, and already the seeds of doubt that he can succeed in holding him off are pouring through the chieftain's mind. He is gathering his thoughts, readying himself for one huge physical effort that he hopes will see him push Feardorcha off him when he notices the pulsation spread itself to every part of his aggressor's face. It is as though there is something mischievously pumping inside the head that is so close to him. Initially, Iarla thinks this little more than a facial reaction to that mounting northern wind which has begun to blow across the fort. But now a violent throbbing of Feardorcha's lips and the beginnings of mutation start to reveal themselves before Iarla's widening eyes.

The O'Brien concentrates his every effort, physical and mental, on summoning his strength into his arms. Then, tightening his grip on each end of his sword, he pushes hard against the weight that is ever-pressing on him. At first, it seems the effort will be futile and, just as he is about to relent, he senses that the pressure which Feardorcha has exerted has eased a little. He looks hard into the dark lieutenant's face. The metamorphosis is in full flow and Feardorcha's attention is obviously divided between Iarla and the transmutation that is happening within his own body. A row of gnarled protrusions seems to course erratically beneath the skin of the oppressor's face and, increasingly, the chieftain realises that the image before him bears very little resemblance to that which was there only minutes earlier. And the wind sweeps even harder across the fort.

As the pressure being exerted by Feardorcha eases off a little more again, Iarla realises that he must take his chance. Summoning all his might, he draws his right knee up hard into his assailant's groin and almost simultaneously pushes him away. So great has been the effort that Iarla has succeeded in driving his opponent back with even more success than he had anticipated. Feardorcha is jettisoned across the centre of the fort, driven right into the path of the fire, and beyond. Embers are seen to scatter in all directions, their burning redness carried on the wind's fanning wings, their brightness all the more enhanced by the darkness of the night against them. And now the mound of blackness that is Feardorcha lies inert on the ground just beyond the place of burning.

Iarla cannot tell whether what he feels can be termed relief or if his greater emotion is some sense of optimistic caution. He eases himself away from the earthen bank and comes slowly towards the spot where his adversary lies. He has taken little more than six or seven paces when the huddled mound appears to momentarily gyrate and then lie still again. Iarla is halted in his tracks. He waits a while to see if there is further movement, then continues his approach. And as he does so, the sweeping wind turns into a violent and swirling vortex, catching leaves and twigs and anything not grounded up into its anger. The embers of the fire are sent to every corner of the earth and Iarla himself is forced to crouch low to avoid being taken in the maelstrom. Then, as quickly as it has come, the gust is gone and all is quiet. As the chieftain stands, the dove flies out again from amidst the branches and comes to rest near that point where the now dead Riordan had identified the entrance to the souterrain.

Iarla's eyes have followed the bird in flight and, just as it has landed, a second gyration from the huddled mound – this time accompanied by a wild and shrilling howl – regains his immediate attention. And as the chieftain shifts his gaze, rising from that spot where Feardorcha had fallen is a creature hideous to behold. Iarla is astounded at what it is he sees reveal itself before his eyes. It is the same animal of darkness that not one full day before had defiled the Lady Sorcha within the sanctity of the monastery walls. It has hooves and yet, as if by contradiction, it has claws and lines of muscle stand out boldly on its neck. The chieftain makes to move even closer, but then, suddenly, some unidentified element deep within him cautions him against doing so.

Now on all fours and blacker than the night, the animal turns its head towards Iarla and growls. It is a growl that is long and gnarled and threatening, and, as the sound makes its way out into the dank night air, two fangs stretch themselves long and white from the creature's mouth. And the young O'Brien instinctively backs away a little. The animal turns again, looks towards the muddy mound beneath which lies the body of Prince Dermot, and then moves slowly towards it. And Iarla waits and watches that very spot where earlier he had committed his father to the earth. Once at the place of burial, the creature initially paws softly at the mud-heap, but then a quickening and violence of movement seems to possess it. Now it flails indiscriminately at the mound, sending swathes of mud in all directions. So rapid is its movement that, in no time at all, the body of Prince Dermot is unearthed and Iarla sees the claws of the beast's forepaws tear into his father's inert flesh.

"Nooooooo!" cries Iarla, and he surges forward, wielding his sword in his fighting arm as he rushes towards the animal. Immediately the creature shifts its attention to the oncoming chieftain and throws itself back onto its hindlegs, so that now it stands at almost twice the height of

The O'Brien. Just as Iarla comes within its reach, the beast sweeps its forepaw out across its own shadow and catches the young man on the face. The claws tear deep into the chieftain's flesh and he is knocked to the ground. Before Iarla has time to even realise he has been hit, the animal has pounced upon him and is working its snout hard against the leader's jaw, trying with all its might to force Iarla's head back. And eventually the young man relents in his resistance. His neck lies bare and open to the aggressor's fangs and he knows that he no longer has the strength to fight.

The animal throws back its head and the whiteness of its long and dagger-like incisors are caught in what light there is. But suddenly there is light upon that light, and all within the fort is as bright as if it were day itself. And the dove that hitherto had rested at the mouth of the souterrain hovers overhead. It is as though the bird is stilled mid-air and a radiance that is blinding exudes from it. The creature stares up transfixed and, as it does so, the dove lowers itself again onto the souterrain and now all the light that it emits is from its eyes. And its eyes are balls of white and they are sharper than the eyes of any other being, and the animal knows that these are eyes that it has seen before. Then, from within the body of the dove emerges the monk Benignus. It is he now who stands at the mouth of the passageway and the onlooking beast sees its greatest fear confirmed.

"Go, Master Iarla," Benignus says quite calmly, still holding the dark one with his stare.

Iarla hesitates in his movement, uncertain of what it is that's happening, bewildered as to who may be this man who has transformed from dove to human before his very eyes. His gaze shifts to the creature and he sees that it is still immobilised, still within the hold of this strange phenomenon.

"There is a ship that leaves this midnight from the harbour wall in Galway, bound for the port of Genoa in the land of Italy," says Benignus. "It will take the Lady Sorcha from these shores, never to return perhaps."

Alarm in Iarla's eyes. Sorcha. Italy. Never to return!

"There is still time, my friend. Now go," the monk says, and, still holding his stare hard against Feardorcha, he steps away from the mouth of the souterrain. There is a momentary hesitation on Iarla's part. He looks to the animal, but its interest in the chieftain has been arrested and it is totally engaged by the strangeness of power that the old monk now holds over it.

"Go. In the name of the O'Brien," orders Benignus, and there is no more resistance. Iarla stands at the opening to the underground passage and raises one of the lighted torches which earlier had been brought into the fort by one or other soldier in Feardorcha's ranks. He looks at Benignus, then at the creature who had been Feardorcha, then at the monk again. They hold their stare, one against the other, neither of them turning to meet the chieftain's eyes.

"Be gone, Iarla of the O'Brien, and may the good Lord Jesus Christ spare you in your journey north," Benignus says, and, before his speech is finished, Iarla has crouched low and extended the flaming torch into the souterrain, throwing light on dark within the passageway. And he is gone.

Still light on dark for a time unmeasured within the fort itself. Good on Evil. Feardorcha knows the power of the brightness that beams upon him. He realises the damage that Benignus might have done to him in the monastery cell had Abbot Nilus not intervened when he did. But equally he knows, because he is of evil, that one can never fully defeat the other. It is the order of things that it should be so. Each has its way and to each its way is right. But neither can exist without the shadow of the other. And they hold their stare.

* * *

Iarla stabs the head of the lighted torch into the ground as he nears the exit from the souterrain. What light the night can throw must be sufficient for him now. He eases his head out of the hole until his eyes have cleared the level of the grass and looks ahead of him. All seems clear. And to his right and left, other than a number of horses that stand in sheltered corners of the field, there seems no sign of danger. Then he turns and sees Feardorcha's men seated here and there on the grass between the fort and the point where he has exited the souterrain. Thank goodness for that, he thinks. His greatest fear as he had travelled through the underground passage had been that, on his exit, he might still have had to negotiate avoiding Feardorcha's troops. Or, worse again, that he might have exited right into their midst. And the horses! Now he knows that fortune has surely smiled its grace upon him.

Iarla reaches his arms upwards, then draws his elbows back down against the earth and levers himself out of the hole. He crouches low, looking right and left, then glances back towards Feardorcha's men. Despite the openness of the terrain, they are oblivious to anything but the banter in which they are engaged. Then the chieftain eyes the distant horses and scurries in their direction.

Within the fort, there are the beginnings of yet another change. Feardorcha, the creature, now appears to cringe submissively beneath Benignus' lighted gaze. The animal huddles into itself, seeming somehow to become much smaller in its size than before. But Benignus knows what this may be. He knows submission is no more in Feardorcha's nature than ever it had been in that of Darkon at the time of the seer Sobharthan and her father Emlik, when they and their people had lived by Loughrask's shores some fifteen hundred years before this time ...

Sobharthan – daughter of Emlik: Emlik – son of Relco;
Relco – father of Darkon: Darkon – brother of Emlik;
Emlik – father of Sobharthan. Sobharthan – the Seer.
She turned slowly, for slowly turns the Circle.
And, like the Circle, there can be no end.

And Benignus knows whence the gift of vision has come down to him. The seer's eyes are of the eternal Circle. They see within, they see without. They see, with equal sight, the then, the now and the morrow.

And Feardorcha too knows whence it is that he has come and that, like Benignus, that which he brings to the world is also indestructible.

So small now is the creature that is Feardorcha that it would seem unthinkable to any unknowing of the powers of darkness that this could possibly be the same vicious beast who had defiled the Lady Sorcha and savagely torn into the flesh of her loved one. And Benignus looks on. And Benignus waits. Huddled into a form that might easily fit into the broadened hand of the now dead Riordan, there is a movement that seems more an involuntary flutter than it is one of any great intent. More movement then, and even more again. And a shape is seen to grow upon itself, and wings are spread, then close again, and an elongated beak stretches from the mouth of the burgeoning creature, and it is heron. Heron. The monk, Benignus, is startled by what he knows to have happened. And the light that fills his eyes begins to fade a little.

The creature that is Feardorcha, that is now bird, is fully formed. It looks around with its all-seeing orb. But unlike any time till now, this heron's gaze is not of good, and Evil knows the victory it has won. And the light that, up to this, had so strongly exuded from Benignus' eyes draws back entirely into him and the holy man bows his head. The old monk is spent. He will not see another year and when, in time, he passes from this earthly world, his spirit will abide and will eventually occupy the soul of one not yet known to any. And it will be a time when powers of Good and Evil ebb and flow, as ever, and still do battle with each other.

The heron cackles out its sound into the night, spreads its wings a second time and, with but little effort, eases itself from the ground. Within the time that it might take to turn one's hand, it is at the height of the greatest of the trees that surround the fort and, in its loping movement, the mighty bird circles the settlement three times, then heads north towards the waters of the bay.

16

Both horse and rider teem with sweat as they near the lakeshore of Loch a' tSáile. They are within minutes of the port of Galway. Iarla's race against time from the battlefield at Corcomroe has blinded him to things that he would ordinarily notice. His memory of the fishing village at Kinvara and, further east of that, the little hamlet where St. Colgan built his churchyard are, at best, hazy. It is only because of the coolness of the waters splashing up against his body, as his steed galloped north through Clarin stream and again at the great freshwater spring that lends its name to Oranmore, that his recall of their adjacent hamlets is more vivid in his mind.

Already Iarla has passed that knob of land that juts out into the lake and points from the town of Galway to the nearby headland of Rinn Mhór. Against the light of night, he can see the masts and sails of ships within the harbour. A little nearer now along the dirt track and he can hear the cries of sailors in some foreign tongue and, in the distance, he discerns sheets of light-coloured canvas move out across the water. It is this mixture of sound and vision that strikes alarm into his heart.

Man and horse round the final bend that will lead them to the harbour wall and Iarla fights the thought that his greatest fears may be confirmed by what it is that he is seeing. A large four-masted cargo ship moves gracefully from dock and, on land, those who have come to attend to its departure are seen to walk from the water's edge.

Iarla, already half-dismounted, arrives at speed into the midst of the four or five who are walking from the dockside. The unexpectedness of his approach sends them scurrying in various directions so as to avoid collision with the onrushing animal. As the chieftain's feet make contact with the ground and he releases his grip on the reins, the horse trundles on for many tens of strides before coming to a halt.

"The ship, sir, the ship, where is she bound?" asks the panting Iarla of one of those who has been at pains to avoid the danger of being felled. He has no way of knowing that he to whom he has addressed his question is none other than Richard le Blake.

Le Blake is less than pleased at the scare given to him and his company, and he is doubly offended by what he perceives to be an impertinence on young Iarla's part.

"What is it to you, man, where she's bound or what and who she may carry beneath her sails?" rasps le Blake rebukingly.

"Please, sir," says Iarla, his pleading tone now winning greater favour with the nobleman, "is it the vessel bound for the port of Genoa?"

"None other, sir," replies le Blake. "The *Bella Donna*, under the steady and masterly stewardship of her captain Giacamo Annelli."

"And Sorcha – the Lady Sorcha – is she on board?"

Le Blake's reaction to the question is a mixture of surprise and apprehension, and Iarla is quick to notice this.

"She is my betrothed, sir," says Iarla assertively. "I am Iarla of Dermot of the Clan O'Brien. Now, please tell me is she on board?"

This time surprise is the only element discernible in le Blake's reaction.

"Well, yes, she is, but –"

And before he has time to finish what he is saying, Iarla has headed at speed down the harbour wall.

"Sorcha," he roars. "Sorcha-a-a-a-a-a." It is only the iron barrier separating the stone pier head from the water that brings Iarla to a halt. "Sorcha," he roars again.

"Iarla," comes the response. It seems faint at first and the chieftain is not altogether sure that he has heard it or if it is more something that his heart wishes he might hear.

"Iarla," the call comes a second time, and this time there is no doubting the single word. And he tightens his eyes against the dark of night and, whether vision or something else, he believes he can discern the white-clad figure of his loved one come to the stern of the ship and reach her hand out towards him.

"Sorcha," he calls, his own hand now stretched in her direction, "I will come for you. I will come for you." And as the words leave his lips, salted tears run down his cheeks and make their way into the corners of his mouth.

The O'Brien leans hard against the barrier at pier's end and looks out upon the churned white surf that dances on the afterwash. "I will come for you," he says again, but this time the words are said more as though into his own heart than out against the night. And Iarla reaches his hand in under his breastplate, then beneath his tunic, and he locates the pouch which his father had given him before going into battle. He undoes the pouch's knotted leather thong and removes what seems to be a stone from within. He holds the object out from him and the white thrown by the turbulence of surf sheds light upon it and he sees that it is amber. His father's words – that Iarla himself might one day pass this very stone on to his own son – come to the young man's mind. Then, he looks out again at the departing vessel.

"Sorcha," he roars again, and, with all his might, he hurls the semi-precious stone in the direction of the ship. He has no way of knowing whether or not the amber heirloom reaches its target, but, aboard the vessel, the Lady Sorcha stoops low to pick up something she has heard falling on the seasoned boards of the ship's deck.

Then suddenly, onshore, Iarla is startled by the low flight of a wide-winged seabird that comes from somewhere almost directly behind him and follows in the wake of the *Bella Donna*. His eyes trace the creature's path until he sees it come to rest on the handrail at the ship's stern. And perched alongside where Iarla thinks his beloved Sorcha is standing, the bird cackles its own definitive sound out into the night. And now he can tell that what he sees is heron.

TERROR ON THE BURREN
by
Ré Ó Laighléis
(ISBN 0-9532777-0-4)

This multiple award-winning and critically acclaimed novel is a superlative mix of the supernatural and the real. Set against the archaeological and geological richness of the Burren landscape in Ireland's County Clare, the author weaves a mesmeric and multi-layered tale of barbarity and beauty, of the imaginative and intrigue, of good and evil.

"Measured, even against his own already high standards, Ré Ó Laighléis has given us an exceptional work of beauty and terror here. This, quite simply, stands apart." **C. J. Haughey, former Taoiseach**

"Another example of Ó Laighléis' shining creations ... Undoubtedly, Ó Laighléis is a gifted writer and we wait with hungry curiosity to see what he will come up with next."
Tom Widger, *The Sunday Tribune*

"You'll never look at the Burren in the same way after you read this tale ... Anyone even slightly intrigued by alternatives to the 20th century's blueprint for living will find this account of life in 200 BC enchanting ... The whole saga unfolds within a slim 114 pages, with the mystical beauty of the Burren permeating every page."
Sharon Diviney, *Ireland on Sunday*

"This is an unusual work of rich and cinematographic prose, a work of excellence in the fantasy genre and one which bears the scope of The Mists of Avalon.*"* **Gabriel Rosenstock, Writer**

"Though ostensibly set on the Burren in the period of prehistory, Ó Laighléis' horrific story of destruction is inextricably connected to more recent murky happenings."
**Prof. Mícheál Mac Craith,
National University of Ireland, Galway**

"A brilliant and fascinating read, which will hold you enthralled to the very end." **Geraldine Molloy, *The Big Issues***

"This is epic story-telling at its very best." **Tony Hickey, *Village***

HOOKED
by
Ré Ó Laighléis
(ISBN 0-9532777-1-2)

Ó Laighléis' highly acclaimed novel tells the horrific and gruelling tale of teenager Alan's slide into the world of drug addiction and his involvement with its murky and danger-filled underworld. Equally importantly, *Hooked* also relates the parents' story: Sandra's world is thrown into turmoil, first by the realisation that her 17-year-old son is in the throes of heroin addiction and then by the discovery of her husband's infidelity. There are no ribbons wrapped around the story here – it is hard, factual and written with sensitivity and skill.

"*It is a riveting story based on every parent's nightmare.*"
Lorna Siggins, *The Irish Times*

"*Ó Laighléis deftly favours creating a dark side of urban life over sledge-hammering the reader with 'Just Say No' messages; the horrors of heroin addiction are revealed within the story itself and, thankfully, the author avoids any preachy commentary.*" **Educationmatters**

"Hooked *inhabits the world of well-off middle-class Dublin ... with all its urban angst, moral decay, drug addiction, loneliness and teen attitudes and problems.*"
Patrick Brennan, *Irish Independent*

"*Ré Ó Laighléis speaks the language of those for whom* Hooked *will strike a familiar chord. If it makes people stop and think – as it undoubtedly will – it will have achieved more than all the anti-drug promotional campaigns we could ever begin to create.*"
News Focus, *The Mayo News*

"*Ó Laighléis deftly walks that path between the fields of teenage and adult literature, resulting in a book that will have wide appeal for both young and older readers.*" **Paddy Kehoe, *RTÉ Guide***

"*The book pulls no punches and there are no happy endings.*"
Colin Kerr, *News of the World*

ALSO AVAILABLE FROM MÓINÍN

ECSTASY
and other stories
by
Ré Ó Laighléis
(ISBN 0-9532777-9-8)

This acclaimed collection looks at the rise, the fall and the versatility
of the human spirit, touching, as it does, on almost every aspect of
human trial and existence. Though unflinchingly hard-hitting, it is
utterly compelling and written with great insight and sensitivity.
Ó Laighléis' greatest gift is that he is a masterful story-teller.

*"This combination of style and tone provides a maturity which rarely
characterises writing targeted mainly at a teenage readership ...
It deserves the widest possible audience."*
Robert Dunbar, *The Irish Times*

*"Always there is an appropriate honed-down style that presents the
narratives in crystal clear detail ... Not just a book for teenagers, but
for everyone who appreciates first-class writing."*
Tony Hickey, *Village*

*"Ó Laighléis is not one for the soft option. He deals unflinchingly with
major social issues that affect all our lives and deals with them with
profound insight and intelligence ... It is Ó Laighléis' creative imagination
that gives the collection its undeniable power. The economy of his prose
allows for no authorial moralising."* **Books Ireland**

*"Ecstasy and other stories is brilliantly written and an eye-opener
for us all as to what could happen if life takes that one wrong turn.
Ré Ó Laighléis is a master of his craft."*
Geraldine Molloy, *The Big Issues*

*"Ecstasy is evocative of the filmography of Ken Loach, and its
minimalistic story-telling, with its sparse and essential style,
constitutes an extraordinarily expressive force."*
Mondadori, Milan, Italy (publishers)

*"The short stories of Ecstasy ... take us, in the Irish context, into new
thematic territories and, more importantly, pay their characters (and, by
extension, their readers) the compliment of allowing them to live with the
consequences of their own choices: complex circumstances are always seen
to defy easy outcomes."*
Books, *The Irish Times Weekend Supplement*

ALSO AVAILABLE FROM MÓINÍN

HEART OF BURREN STONE
A collection of short stories
by
Ré Ó Laighléis
(ISBN 0-9532777-2-0)

National and international award-winning author Ré Ó Laighléis gives us a collection that is disturbingly provocative, yet permeated throughout by a humane and perceptive sensitivity. His stories alternate between the serious and witty. Set against both urban and rural backgrounds, these stories range in location from England to the United States and from France to Ireland North and South, with a concentration on the Burren.

Ó Laighléis is equally adept whether handling the loss of childhood innocence in cosmopolitan Dublin or remotest rural Ireland, the depravity that, at times, replaces such innocence in adult years, or the twists in life that determine happiness and misery. His characters bear all the frailty and vulnerability that epitomise the difficulty of survival in contemporary society.

Whether the tragicomedy of two nine-year-olds arguing their political corners on the North of Ireland's Garvaghy Road, the conniving roguery of a Burren publisher or the pain-filled dilemma of a dying cancer patient in a Boston hospital appealing to be assisted on his way – there is an unnerving universality to Ó Laighléis' writing.

ALSO AVAILABLE FROM MÓINÍN

THE GREAT BOOK OF THE SHAPERS:
A right kick up in the Arts
by
Ré Ó Laighléis
(ISBN 0-9532777-8-X)

In a world where there are fewer true artists than there are mere pretenders and where the ordinary citizen is disenfranchised, yet has to subsidise the indulgences and affectations of poseurs and shapers, these would-be artists are so far up their own ends that they are coming out of their mouths – and sometimes, it would nearly seem, out of others' mouths.

Ó Laighléis bursts the bubble on the 'let's-say-nothing' culture of pretence, as the ubiquitous and ever-overseeing Fly tee-hees his way throughout the hilarity of it all.

This satirical look at a pretentiousness in the arts that feeds upon itself really is 'let's-call-a-spade-a-shovel' territory.

"This latest novel, his eighth, again highlights Ó Laighléis' remarkable versatility."
CORKnow

"It is a farcical tirade against the hangers-on, the spoofers, the plámásers and the lickspittles that gravitate towards the arts: hoisted up on their own petard, they succeed in disenfranchising both themselves and the man-on-the-street from the arts world."
Mark Keane, The Clare People

"Ó Laighléis satirises the pretentious in the hope that some sanity may return to our appreciation of what is culturally sound, and that we judge things for what they really are and not what they pretend to be."
'Book of the Week', Galway Independent

"Art and art form are lost, while characters lose themselves with their own sense of importance."
Aingeal Ní Mhurchú, The Southern Star